"Mary Lapp, is that you?"

Amos called around the balaclava that was protecting his nose from the biting winter air.

He stopped his buggy beside her and hopped down. All she could manage was a simple hello.

"Oh, don't look so mortified." Amos laughed at her. "I am not one to judge you. There has been a lot of gossip, but I like to give people the opportunity to explain themselves, though you most certainly do not need to explain to me. It is just nice to see you."

"Nice to see you, too," she admitted, blushing as he tucked a strand of her hair back under the cap she had worn to keep her head warm. His touch was electrifying and just then she was reminded that she had always liked Amos. Something about him had always pulled her in and intrigued her, but *rumspringa* had got in the way, and then everything else.

"You coming back home or just going to visit your parents?" he asked.

"I am not sure which just yet," she replied.

Hannah Schrock is the bestselling author of numerous Amish romance and Amish mystery books.

THE LOST LITTLE
AMISH BOY

Hannah Schrock

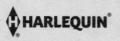

ISBN-13: 978-1-335-49005-6

The Lost Little Amish Boy

First published in 2018 by Burton Crown Ltd.
This edition published in 2020.

Recycling programs
for this product may
not exist in your area.

This edition published by arrangement with Harlequin Books S.A.

For questions and comments about the quality of this book,
please contact us at CustomerService@Harlequin.com.

Harlequin Enterprises ULC
22 Adelaide St. West, 40th Floor
Toronto, Ontario M5H 4E3, Canada
www.Harlequin.com

Printed in U.S.A.

THE LOST LITTLE
AMISH BOY

Prologue

Mary looked at herself in the mirror. Englisch clothes did look really good on her.

"Are you coming?" Anna asked for the millionth time. "You have been staring at yourself for so long."

Mary giggled and took a deep breath before she took her kapp off. This was the first time in her entire eighteen years of life that she would be going out with her long brunette hair uncovered. It took a moment of getting used to that thought before she could actually take it off.

"Yeah," Anna said, coming up behind her, and rested a hand on her shoulder. "It was hard for me the first time too."

Mary smiled nervously at her before she pulled her kapp off. Her hair was in a bun and it held its place, but Anna smiled and loosened the restricting hairpins that kept it up. Mary watched her reflection as her hair cascaded over her shoulders and down her back. For good measure, Anna ran her fingers through it and threw some strands over her shoulder. Looking at her reflection, Mary could barely identify the meek young woman she had always been. The one who had been too shy to even step outside her house most days. Before her stood a different girl. Her green eyes set into her heart-shaped face were now framed by gorgeous flowing brunette hair. She always knew she was pretty, and the boys in the community had never spared a moment telling her just that, but for the first time in her life the only word that came to her mind was *beautiful*.

"Let's go," Anna whispered in her ear, pulling her hand as they exited the halfway house for Amish children that they were staying in.

This was Mary's first time outside of her community. Anna had been to the Englisch world a couple of times before, because her family had an ice-cream business that regularly required she make trips for certain supplies. The experience was not as daunting for her as it was for Mary who came from a neighboring Amish community that had far stricter rules.

Nevertheless, Mary smiled as they walked the Englisch streets, looking at her reflection every chance she got. The experience was exhilarating.

"Where are we going?" she asked Anna.

Anna smiled and pointed up ahead where a group of people stood loitering before what looked to be a huge shopping mall. Mary could recognize a couple of them from her community and realized these were other young people using their rumspringa break to experience the Englisch world. She only recognized three of the eight people there. The other faces were new. One in particular caught her attention, and as he smiled across at her, Anna introduced him as an Englisch boy by the name of Robert.

She smiled nervously at him. She had a feeling she was going to enjoy her trip here.

An Adventurous Spirit

Three months later

Ruth woke engulfed in the silence of her house. Most mornings it was just another day, but today she wished something else would greet her ears. She wished she woke to a tiny face poking through her door or crawling into bed with her and Samuel, much as it had been when she was younger.

It had been five years since she and Samuel were married. Five long years, and still Gott had not seen it fit to bless them with a child. She had prayed. She had prayed many days and nights, but still nothing. It wasn't that their marriage was lacking, that was most certainly not the case. It was just that after five years, she felt like it was time. It was once suggested to her that she seek the answer medically in the Englisch world, but she knew better than to hang on to that as any form of hope. Gott's will. That was the rule she lived with. That was the rule they all lived with. It would either happen or it wouldn't. Whatever Gott had decided.

"Morning," Samuel said, rolling over in bed and smiling up at her. He ran a hand along her back and fell back asleep.

She smiled down at him before getting out of bed. Soon he would be up and getting ready for the fields. Completing her personal morning rituals, she made her way downstairs to the kitchen. Humming as she started breakfast, Samuel came down the stairs a few minutes later and wrapped his arms around her.

"I love you," he whispered into her kapp.

"Love you more." She smiled. She knew he meant every word of it. He had made it his point of duty to show her he did every chance he got.

"Did you hear about your cousin?" he asked. His eyes widened with a twinkle.

She glared at him knowing exactly where he was going to go with the conversation, but she didn't think it was that funny at all.

"Come on," he teased her. "We can't say we didn't know that was going to happen."

She jabbed at him with the fork in her hand. "Anna is a sweet child. I knew nothing of the sort."

"Right," Samuel chuckled. "I am happy for her in a strange way. She was always a bit more than this community could hold."

Ruth smiled with a sigh. She had to admit that her eighteen-year-old cousin had always been quite the handful. She had a kind of adventurous spirit that wouldn't have survived too well in the community. She had always broken harmless rules with utmost respect, if that was possible. She chuckled at the thought. Now the gossip her husband was referring to was that Anna had gone to the Englisch world on rumspringa and decided that was where she wanted to stay. With any other child, one might think that was just temporary, but with Anna, Ruth knew better. The Englisch world wouldn't hold her back and force her to conform to a way of life that she did not naturally adapt to. She knew if she was ever to talk to Anna, the young woman would profess her love for her community and humble way of life.

They all knew she loved it there, but she had always craved more. There she went, having more.

"Her friend Mary came back, though," Samuel said around a mouthful of eggs.

Ruth was about to ask him how he knew that, given that Mary was from the neighboring community, but she didn't bother. News like that travelled fast. Nothing much by way of excitement happened in their communities. That was understandable, given that they were a simple people living simple lives; when a young person went on rumspringa and didn't come back, news travelled fast because of the implications on the family.

"Good for her," Ruth said, smiling. "At least her parents won't be sick with worry about her."

"Well," Samuel said, "I don't think you and your aunt and uncle should be too worried about Anna. I am not, because she knows she can always come home if it doesn't work out, and I know she will be just fine."

"In all your gossiping, did you get an idea of where she might be staying?" Ruth rolled her eyes at him.

Samuel looked away with a guilty grin and all but whispered the apartment details he had heard Anna had taken residence in.

"Unbelievable," Ruth said to him as he kissed her cheeks and made his escape out the door.

She stared after him as his sturdy strong figure ran down the few steps of the porch and to the fields. She loved him more than life, but if he thought she would take it so easy when they had a child who ran off, he had another thing coming. In fact, she knew if that happened, she would be inclined to march into the Englisch world and take her child back. She knew she wouldn't, but she would be worried sick.

But first she needed to actually have a child…

With that thought, she went back to the kitchen, cleaned up after her husband and then saw to the other chores. By the time she was done, she had a few hours before he would be back for lunch. She thought of going by the schoolhouse where she helped out most days, but the emotional aching for a child of her own was not going to make that an easy task today. She instead decided to bake. But first she decided to take a few minutes to write a quick letter to her cousin. She wished her well but let it be known that home was always here for her. She had seen quite a few young Amish make the decision to leave the community during their youth, but it rarely lasted long. In fact she could only remember two instances where those that left did so for good. In both of those cases their families had shut them out the minute they had declared their wishes. This was why she had penned her letter in a gentle tone. Wish them well but pray that they return and make it easy for them to do so. She hoped her aunt and uncle were taking the same approach, she knew that they must be worried sick. She wondered about calling on them, but no doubt they would have a constant stream of visitors at the moment, when all they would probably want to do was sit and cry. She decided that she would leave her visit for the moment and turned her attention to the kitchen.

Kitchen therapy was what she called it. She could make a few extra dollars selling her pastries to the ice-cream shop, as she so often did. With that in mind, she tuned everything else out and focused on what she was making. By the time Samuel came back from the fields, she was in higher spirits. After lunch she made her way to the community barn, where women would be making noodles and gossiping about what little there was to gossip about.

On a normal day that would not have intrigued her, but she could use the distraction today.

Rainbows and Unicorns

Mary stared at herself in her bedroom mirror. Seems staring at herself had become her new favorite pastime. The problem was, this time it wasn't with good thoughts in her head. She sighed solemnly and tied her kapp around her head. Just three months earlier she had been sighing and taking it off with a much more laissez-faire attitude.

A week ago, she had come back to the Amish community. The Englisch world had offered her many things, but as time went by, she found she missed the little creek that ran at the edge of the forest, she missed harvesting season and the fun she had with her friends while they stormed the apple and orange orchards, she missed waking up to her mother's kisses on her forehead. She was eighteen, and for eighteen years her mother had been waking her up the same way every day. She missed arguing about just about anything with her father. Some arguments were heated discussions about life aimed at strengthening her convictions and others aimed at teaching her a thing or two. Then there were the arguments every child had with their parents. What she missed most was the hot cup of chocolate and a warm hug that he always had for her at the end of the day.

She missed the little things she didn't have in the Englisch world, and the more she thought about never having them again, the more it scared her. When the melancholy had set in in ways she could no longer ignore, she had looked at the ease with which the Englisch world suited Anna. She had watched her best friend go job hunting and even helped her to settle into her new apartment. Looking at the relatively cheap loft space Anna was in, Mary had only thought of how unlike home it was.

A week later here she was, but it wasn't all rainbows and unicorns anymore.

"Mary!" her mother called. "Don't tell me you went back to sleep. Soon your friends will come to my door hollering for you and I will have to run them all off."

Mary laughed. "I am up, Mamm! No need to get the broomstick out."

She could hear her mother's soft chuckle floating up the stairs to soothe her.

"We know how she loves that broomstick," her father said, stepping out of his room as she made her way down.

They laughed as they sat at the breakfast table. She could see how happy they were to have her back. Nothing could replace the joy she was experiencing at this minute, and she hoped nothing would. They ate breakfast and finished just as the first chorus of voices called to her from outside.

"Mary! Will you come out before your mother gets us with that old broomstick?"

Her parents laughed.

"Go!" her mother said, handing her the lunch she had packed for her. Her father kissed her cheeks as she went through the door.

"If you don't stop, I might just get her a new one to bat at you with," Mary said to Joshua as she skipped down the stairs.

He giggled and hugged her as his girlfriend and her closest friend, Bethany, came to join them. They chatted about so many things in the few minutes it took for them to get to Joshua's parents' farm. His father had died a few months before Mary made her sojourn into the Englisch world. Since then the girls helped when it was time for planting. Joshua had a few farm hands in to help with the heavier tasks, but the farm was small enough for his friends to help with everything else. That afternoon they would be helping with a barn-raising. The girls had volunteered to help varnish the wood that would be used on the inside and porch areas. It was one of Mary's favorite community activities.

"You okay?" Bethany whispered to her as they placed young tomato plants from their seeding trays into the ground.

"Yes," she answered a little more rushed than she intended to. "Why?"

Bethany smiled. "You just seemed a bit preoccupied. Don't tell me you miss the Englisch world."

"Oh no!" she exclaimed. "I miss Anna, but not the Englisch world at all."

"And that cute Englisch boy you wrote me about?" Bethany asked with a grin.

Mary blushed and passed it off as something in the moment. Truth was that she much preferred Amish men anyway. There was an ease and familiarity about Amish men that she was attracted to. Robert was indeed handsome and had made her time in the Englisch world more fun, but she didn't miss him at all.

"You gained some weight there," Bethany pointed out. "Your cheeks are getting a little plump too."

"That's a good thing," Joshua called back. "She was all skin and bone before she left here. Maybe we should send her back."

Bethany laughed as Mary threw a handful of dirt at him. Mary laughed but the anxiety she had been feeling all day returned. The easy, pointless chatter that usually accompanied their time together didn't really register for most of the day. She laughed and giggled as she went about her chores, but she was distracted and with good cause.

"Mary Lapp! Come here!" The bishop's wife called to her as she was about to leave the barn-raising later that evening. She shyly walked into the woman's open arms.

"It is nice to have you back," the woman whispered as she hugged her. "Oh, you gained a couple of pounds too. Especially in the middle section."

Mary laughed nervously. "I did."

"It looks good on you," the older woman said before pinching her cheeks and walking off.

Mary was about to have a full-blown panic attack, and she made her excuses to Bethany and Joshua and ran home. Halfway home, she turned down the hill and made her way to the Englisch pharmacy a half a mile away. Walking with haste before her friends decided to come after her, she left the community and walked the fifteen minutes to the store.

"In a rush today, aren't we?" the old man who ran the place laughed at her.

"Yes," she replied with a smile. A couple of Englischers came in behind her and she was happy for the distraction.

She took a small package from the shelf to the young girl behind the cash register who was wearing so much makeup, Mary momentarily wondered how far below those layers she would have to dig to find her actual skin.

"That's three dollars," the girl said, popping her gum as she spoke.

Mary pulled the money from her pocket and asked for the bathroom. She half expected the girl to make some snide comment, but the young woman didn't seem to care about Mary or what she was buying. She simply pointed Mary in the direction that she needed to go and went back to staring at her phone.

Mary walked briskly down the corridor to the bathroom, closing the door behind her. She looked down at the package she had just bought and prayed that it didn't give the result she was thinking it would. Less than five minutes later, the plus sign materialized on the small stick. She stared at it in disbelief. Almost tripping over herself, she bought two more on her way out. She walked with the same haste back home and into the outhouse. Repeating the process, her heart sank even further.

By her calculations she was a little over three months pregnant and had no idea what she would do. The tears flowing down her cheeks were real and the panic that set in, even more so. She had no money and no way to take care of a child on her own. Even worse was the fact that being pregnant out of wedlock could get her shunned from her ordnung. The same ordnung she had just run back to. But being pregnant was just one part of this, being pregnant with an Englisch man was unforgivable.

It dawned on her then just what she had gotten herself into. She let herself fall apart for the first time in her life. She had no solution to her problem, and she couldn't run to her parents to solve it for her. She thought of how happy they looked that morning and knew that somehow she was about to ruin that.

She had no idea what she would do, so she sat right there and cried her heart out.

Gott decides it is Time

As the rain started, Ruth ran outside in a bid to get the clothes off the line. She could hear Samuel in her head telling her to leave them and not get wet in the downpour. Ever since she was young, she would fall sick the minute she got caught in the rain. She remembered watching longingly as the other children danced in the rain on hot summer days when the downpour was sweet relief, but not her. Her parents quickly scooped her up and dragged her inside, away from all the fun. She had been thinking lately about why it was that she had not become pregnant, maybe it was because she had been so sickly as a child.

The rain picked up and she left the wetter clothes on the line. When it stopped, she would rinse them out again and put them back out.

"Ruth Beiler!" she heard her aunt shouting at her as she walked into the house. "Don't you know not to go out in the rain?"

She sighed as her Aunt Ruthie, after whom she had been named, helped her with the clothes in her arms.

"I just didn't want to have to redo all that washing when the rain passed," she confessed.

"At the expense of your health?" her aunt frowned at her. "You know your constitution is poorly."

Ruth held back a laugh. Her aunt was the only person she knew who spoke of someone's *constitution*. It was always funny to hear, and there were days when she and Samuel would sit on the porch laughing at the funny things people said, and her Aunt Ruthie would always be a subject of that conversation. She loved the woman dearly and so did Samuel, but they couldn't help it.

"My constitution will be just fine," she giggled back.

Her aunt, who had just started graying around the edges of her kapp, scowled at her before making her way to Ruth's stove.

"What do you have boiling here?" she asked Ruth.

Ruth looked at the woman who reminded her so much of her mother who had passed away four years before.

"Just some soup," she answered, moving the bed linen to the couch in the next room and folding it. The fact that her aunt had asked about food, and it was just before mid-afternoon, meant the woman would be sharing the meal and likely wouldn't be leaving until a bit later. Ruth didn't mind. On days like the ones she had been having lately, she welcomed the company.

"Where is that young man of yours?" her aunt asked.

"In the fields. He will be going down to the market to drop some goods off before he comes back home. So it will be a while."

"Okay," her aunt said, taking a muffin from the fresh

batch on the counter which Mary had just made. "How are you, Ruth?"

She opened the ice box and poured them each a glass of lemonade, trying to figure out how she should respond to her aunt's question. She knew better than to fib, although that was not in her nature.

"I am not sure how I am doing," she finally responded. Taking a muffin, she invited her aunt out onto the front porch, where they could watch the rain and talk.

"I figured," her aunt said, taking a seat beside her. "You haven't been to the schoolhouse in a few days, and that is unlike you. The same thing bothering you?"

"What if I am the reason I haven't had a child yet?" she asked, trying not to allow the frustration to take root.

"You have not had a child yet because Gott does not think it is your time," her aunt replied.

Ruth was getting annoyed at that response, though she clung to her faith and tried to believe it. "That's not what I meant. What if something is wrong with me that I can't be with child? It's time now."

"We can't rush the process. It is your time when it is your time," her aunt replied calmly. "Do you want to go to an Englisch doctor and find out what is wrong?"

"That will never be allowed," she lamented. "I don't want to break rules."

"Well," her aunt sighed, taking her hand. "Think about it. If not, then don't rush the process."

"My house feels empty," Ruth said, tears welling up in her eyes. "I want that to change."

"And things are okay with you and Samuel?"

"Oh, he is perfect!" Ruth replied without hesitation. The thought of her husband stopped the tears.

"Maybe you can think about it together, but don't stay away from the schoolhouse. The children miss your games and cookies."

Ruth smiled and leaned back in the chair. "Everything in its own time, right?"

"Everything when Gott decides it is time that you have it," her aunt corrected her.

She sighed, feeling a little better. They spent the next hour talking about Anna, her daughter. It seemed her aunt was handling it better than Ruth was. She even said she writes to her, as the bishop allows it. Apparently, Anna had decided to try her hand at being a secretary and loved it.

"Has she found an Englisch boy yet?" Ruth joked.

Her aunt laughed. "You know my Anna. She will get there when she is good and ready. Unlike you she has no problem trusting the process."

Ruth giggled. "I would like a bit of her patience. Don't you miss her?"

"All day, every single day," her aunt said with a sigh. "But I am just happy she writes and she is okay. It could have been a case where she ran off and I never heard from her again, so I am happy that she is fine."

That Ruth could understand.

A Bad Romance

A few miles away, Mary was having a hard time eating the breakfast her mother put before her. She explained that she might be coming down with a cold from all the recent rains. Her mother made her a cup of fresh mint tea and packed her lunch.

"Mamm, I will be working at the schoolhouse today. We will be taking the children into the forest for a little fun by the creek, so I might be back a bit late."

Her mother nodded, but Mary knew that wasn't the only reason she would be back late. She felt bad for misleading her parents, but it was necessary. She did what she was to do for the day, but just before she knew they would be ready to leave the creek, she excused herself and went down to the pharmacy where she had bought her pregnancy test. She had made a horrible mistake but she did not want it ruining her life.

She didn't know exactly what she was going to do, but for now she had one plan. She was going to speak to Anna. That was the only plan she had.

"Hello," the old man greeted her again as she entered

the pharmacy. She smiled at him, pulling a chocolate bar from the shelf and going to the cash register.

When the young woman gave her the change, Mary made her way to the bench by the bus station just outside. The pay phone she intended to use was right beside her. She looked at the clock on the church tower across the street and waited. It was a few minutes after five. In her letters, Anna said she got home by half past five every day. Mary was going to call her cell phone when she knew she might be home. She couldn't risk Anna being around the others when she called.

Five minutes later, Anna picked up on the first ring. "Hello?"

"Hey," Mary said nervously.

"Mary!" Anna's voice instantly sounded way more joyous than Mary was feeling. "How are you?"

Not wanting to waste any more time, Mary answered. "Not so good, Anna. Not so good. I am pregnant."

Mary waited for the moment of shock to pass so that Anna could respond. "What did you just say?"

Mary sighed. "I am pregnant, Anna, and I don't know what to do."

"Oh Mary," Anna lamented. All the joy now gone from her voice. "Do your parents know?"

"No, I can't tell them. I will be shunned. They will be embarrassed and so ashamed of me."

"Who is the father, Mary?" Anna asked. Mary could hear the suspicion in her voice.

"I think you know exactly who it is," she replied.

Anna sighed. "So that means you are a few months pregnant."

"Yeah, what do I do? I am not showing just yet, but I will start showing soon. I can't stay here."

"Well, you know you can always come stay with me, but what then? You have to tell your parents eventually."

Mary took solace in the fact that Anna had said *eventually*. Right now, her main concern was not to break their hearts. She would have to leave the community; maybe she could have the baby in secret before she told them that she was pregnant.

"What do I do?" Mary asked, trying not to break down.

"For now, there is only one thing you can do," Anna replied softly. "You can come stay with me and we can figure it out from there. I would advise you to leave before you start showing. You don't want your parents to have to deal with that rumor going around."

"And Robert? I don't think I want him to know."

"Why not?" Anna asked her.

"So many reasons, Anna, we will talk about them when I get to you though."

"Okay," Anna sighed. "When will you leave?"

Mary knew she wouldn't be leaving before she knew that she had no other choice. For now, she would act as if it was just business as usual. When her stomach was about to become obviously extended, she would go. For the first time in a long time, she was happy that her Amish frocks were roomy and not form-fitting.

"Don't worry, Mary," Anna said. "We will figure it out."

Mary sighed and placed all her faith in those few words. A minute later, she hung up and headed home. The skies were dark with the promise of rain and the thunder rumbled gently as if warning of the troubles she would be having in the near future.

"Hey, Mary!" Amos, the carpenter's son, called to her as he passed in his buggy. "Want a lift?"

She gladly accepted and he stepped down to help her up. "We are in for a bit of a shower."

He turned his eyes up to the skies and nodded. "Yes, the later summer rain is always a promise. We could use it."

They chatted about the late summer harvest coming up and when she got to her house, her father was outside reading a magazine. Thanking Amos, she smiled as she walked up the stairs.

"Oh, a boy now, do I see romance on the horizon for my Mary?" her father joked.

Mary blushed and kissed his cheek. "Maybe, Daed. Just maybe."

She hugged her mother before heading up the stairs to get ready for dinner. Sitting at the edge of her bed, she cried. What had she gotten herself into? Now more than ever, she was hoping and praying that it would all work out better than it was looking at the moment. She had to hold on to that hope.

If it didn't, she was going to lose far more than she was prepared to, and far more than she knew how to live without. She couldn't allow that to happen.

A Small Feathery Touch

Mary waited a whole month before she spoke out to her parents. It was a month of practicing her speech in front of the small mirror in her bathroom and wishing she could tell her friends what was going on with her. She couldn't, though. Anna was her sole confidante.

That Saturday evening when her father had come in from work and the dinner had passed with its usual banter, she spoke meekly.

"Mamm, Daed," she said. "There is something I want to talk to you about."

"What is it, Dochder?" her father said, looking at her with concern.

She took a deep breath. "I think I want to go back to the Englisch world for a while," she finally said.

The silence that took over the entire house was deafening. If a smile could literally fall from someone's face, that is exactly what would have happened to her parents. They were usually very chatty, but they seemed to have lost their ability to speak. And Mary didn't know what to say, so she waited.

"Why do you feel you need to go back there?" her mother finally asked.

To her side, her father fidgeted with the food on his plate as if he had just been reprimanded by his mother. In front of her, across the table, her mother stared eagerly at her face, waiting for a response she couldn't give her.

"I love being home," Mary began, knowing the next words out of her mouth would likely have to be a lie to protect her secret. She was trying to hold off on that as long as was possible.

"Then what is it?" her mother begged.

It was at times like this that she wished her parents had other children. The idea of your only child leaving home, possibly never to return, was daunting. If she had siblings, she knew her parents would still love and miss her just as much, but the pressure she was feeling right now might not have been so great.

"I just feel like maybe I made a mistake coming back early. There are things I still miss about that world."

Her father shifted but said nothing. She could feel his gaze penetrating the side of her face. It was as if he was trying to stare down into her soul, and he was doing a mighty fine job of it.

"There is something you are not telling us, Dochder," he said in the patient way only he could.

She took a deep breath for the umpteenth time in the last couple of months and spoke. "I just feel like there are some things I need to sort out there. I also want to spend a bit more time with Anna before I come back and take the vow to completely be part of the church. I won't be able to see her again after that."

She was trying to be as truthful as she could possibly be. The coming back and being part of the church was what she really wanted, but she might never get that opportunity. Right now, she needed to give them and herself a bit of hope.

"When will you leave again?" her father asked, placing emphasis on the last word.

She thought for a minute. To them she was trying to decide, but for her she was just trying to calculate how much longer before she actually had to leave.

"I was thinking I would stay until the autumn harvest and then go and come back after a couple of months."

Her mother got up from the table. "You will miss Christmas."

Mary had thought about that, but she couldn't risk staying longer. She needed to give herself a chance to handle her situation without too much repercussion on her family. If that was going to be a problem, she would miss whatever celebration she would have to. Hopefully only for this year.

"I will be back before you know it, Maem," she pleaded with her mother to understand, but even then, she knew the disappointment was way too much for her mother to process right now.

"Can't you wait until after Christmas?" her mother asked. Mary knew then and there that if she didn't speak with resolution, she would never be able to weasel her way out of this.

Looking up, she met her mother's gaze. "I will leave in a month, Mamm, and I will be back before you know it. I just really want to go as soon as possible. Don't make this harder for all of us than it has to be."

She saw her mother's shoulders sag with resignation and knew she had won a battle that she really didn't need to win at all. The rest of the evening passed by in solemn silence, and as evening fell, she sat on the stairs by the porch looking out.

"I still think there is something you are not telling us," her father said, coming to sit beside her. He never faltered in his understanding. While her mother would give up the rational for emotions, her father had never once faltered. He always made sure she knew that he was there.

"There is, Daed," she said. Feeling a burden lift from her shoulders at the truth of it.

"And you are sure you don't want to? Whatever it is, we can figure it out together as a family," he assured her, taking her hand.

"Not this time, Daed," she said, resting her head on his shoulder. "This is something I have to deal with alone. Just know there is really no other place I would rather be than here with you and Mamm."

"I know that," her father said, kissing her forehead. "Whatever it is, you get it out of the way, and you come back home to us when you are good and ready. Your mother will eventually understand."

"I am coming back home, Daed," she said, looking at him. She wasn't sure how she would just yet, but she knew that one thing for sure. "I am coming back home."

Her father kissed her cheek and squeezed her hand again. Right then she felt her baby's first movements and smiled. It was a small feathery touch from the inside that told her that all would be right in her world.

Leaving to Hide

Another month later and Mary knew she had to leave. There was no way she could stay longer. Her stomach was not the rosy protruding bump of mothers close to delivery, but even in her roomy frock, she was beginning to see evidence of more than the gaining of a couple of pounds. The morning sickness had become more frequent, and even though she tried to hide it from her parents, she knew it would just be a matter of time.

That evening she stole away from her barn chores early and walked to the corner station to use the pay phone. She knew she was progressing far along in her pregnancy because the walk was far more exhausting than it had ever been.

"Mary?" Anna answered the phone with concern in her voice. "I wasn't expecting your call for a couple of days. Is everything okay?"

In the background, Mary could hear phones ringing and she knew she had caught Anna at work.

"Is it a bad time?"

"Of course not! Talk to me," Anna replied.

Mary sighed. "I think it's time, Anna. I won't be able to hide this any longer. My morning sickness is at an all-time high too."

Anna didn't respond for some time. "Well, things are ready for you at my place. You can come whenever you are ready, but Mary?"

"Yeah?"

Anna sighed. It seemed like they had been doing a lot of that lately. "You might want to not give your parents much warning and do it at night when not too many eyes can see you leaving. That will cause them more embarrassment."

Mary had been thinking about all of this, but the truth was that she didn't want to have to do that to her parents. What Anna said made a lot of sense though. Her mother would make a goodbye harder than she was prepared for. She would definitely need to do this under the cloak of darkness.

"Okay," she finally said. "I will leave tomorrow night. Would you be able to meet me at the edge of the fields with a car?"

"Yes," Anna said. "I will be there at 12 midnight."

"Thanks, Anna," Mary whispered, trying hard to stay afloat under the sadness that threatened to drown her. "I don't know how I will ever be able to repay you."

"You never have to," Anna said with a laugh. "This is what friends are for."

Mary hung up feeling a little better, but she knew that sneaking out would be no easy task for her. Her heart would break with every step she took away from the place she most wanted to be, and the two people she loved most. It would be no easy task at all, but she would do it as best as she could.

During her final days there, she spent much time with Joshua and Bethany. She laughed so much that she sometimes thought she might give birth right on the spot. That would really ruin all her plans. The hilarity of that thought alone made her laugh even harder at one of Joshua's jokes that really wasn't that funny.

She was happy. Even though she knew come daylight they wouldn't be seeing her for a very long time. She was happy in those moments, and it made her sad that her child might grow up never experiencing this part of her life with her. Her friends' coddling and her mother spoiling the baby with treats; her father would never get the chance to teach him all the things he had taught her.

She pushed those thoughts to the back of her mind as she headed home to her parents for the last time in a long time.

The smell of her mother's freshly baked goods was the first to catch her nose as she walked into the house. She spent longer than usual with her parents and wanted to enjoy as much of them as she could. When they finally turned in for the night, she made sure not to miss out on the kisses, hugs and I-love-you's. In her father's arms she felt safe, but that was a safety blanket she would have to leave behind. She silently packed a small bag of necessities. There was so much she wanted to take with her in case she couldn't make it back. In fact, if she could pack the entire house into her backpack and take it with her, that is exactly what she would have done.

A few minutes before twelve, she snuck downstairs and packed a few of her mother's muffins into a bag as well as an unopened bottle of lemonade. She had written a letter in the early hours while she waited on them to fall asleep, which she left on the kitchen table. Taking one last breath and a look around, she stepped out into the night air.

"Leaving without a goodbye, Dochder?" Her father's voice greeted her.

Her heart stopped beating for a couple of seconds, but the warming smile on his face was enough to calm her. She should have known better than to think he would not have figured out she would be leaving in the middle of the night.

"Yes, Daed," she said and walked into his outstretched arms.

"Anna will be waiting on you, won't she?" He asked with a smile.

Mary returned it. "Yes, she will."

"Well, at least distance has never changed your friendship. Hold on to that. Whatever you are going through, you will always have us, but you will need a good friend. Cherish her."

"I do, Daed. I do."

They walked in silence to the edge of the rolling fields of the Amish community. Up ahead they could see a car waiting for her. Her father walked her to the door and bent to look at Anna in the back of the car.

"Young lady," he said sternly.

"M-Mr. Lapp?" she stuttered. If one could see a heart in a mouth, that is what one would have seen looking at Anna at that moment.

But Mary watched her father walk around to Anna's door, pull it open and pull her out for a hug.

"Take care of each other, and make sure to write."

A stunned Anna agreed, and Mary's father hugged her one last time before he reluctantly let her climb into the taxi and drive away from him. She looked back until the darkness had completely swallowed him up, then she rested her head on Anna's shoulder and cried.

The Desperate Situation

The first order of business was getting Mary a little job as soon as she arrived in the city. Anna had made it easy for her by lining up some interviews, and while they actively tried to avoid the eyes of the rest of the group they used to hang with, Mary eliminated those where the hours and the pay made no sense. And two weeks later, she settled on one that was easy enough in a small convenience store.

"You know you could work online from home. You probably would never have to leave the house if you didn't want to," Anna pointed out to her.

Mary wasn't sure what 'online' meant exactly, but she thought it would be a good idea given that she was trying to avoid people like Robert. She was just happy that, being naturally petite, her pregnancy did not cause too much of a stir as her baby bump did not grow too big. Anna had asked her if she wanted to know her baby's gender, and so at her first doctor's checkup, she found out it was a boy. That really did help, as it narrowed down the clothes and supplies they would need.

Mary was quietly fitting into the rhythm of her life a few weeks later when one day, Anna posed a question she had thought about only in passing.

"Will you keep the baby, Mary? Or are you going to give him up for adoption?"

Mary froze at the kitchen counter when the question was posed. She was shocked at being asked, but she had thought about it anyway.

"I don't know, Anna," she admitted. "I need this child to have a shot at a good life without condemnation. So, it is a thought."

"Well, Robert and his family moved away. They are in California," Anna said a few moments later.

Mary didn't know how to feel about that, but thought it was probably for the best. He was a year younger than her, and although she was not judging, Englisch men were not accustomed to raising children as young as Amish young men were.

"Maybe that's all for the better," she said. The truth was he should not have to lose his youth because of this either. She rubbed her tummy and thought for a while. Anna left her in silence, and they didn't speak about it again for a few days while Mary settled into her work at the small convenience store run by an older woman everybody called Aunty Jasmine.

That Saturday, Mary sneezed for the third time in that day as she walked through the town. Her nose ached and she could feel a cold coming on yet again. This would be the second time in the weeks since she had arrived in the town that she would be sick.

"I will make you some soup as soon as we get home," Aunty Jasmine said, rubbing her back as she walked into work that day. Never before did she think she would have missed the dry acrid temperatures of the summer, and she was beginning to question her smarts as to why she had chosen to leave the warmth of home and her mother's winter medicinal remedies. The town's doctor had made it clear that she wasn't ailing or suffering from some bug she might have picked up, she was simply adjusting to the thinner and colder air. She wished she would just adjust already. For the sake of the child she was carrying, she hoped she would get better soon.

She smiled in gratitude at Jasmine's suggestion and prayed it would be enough. She had taken in more soup in the last two weeks than she ever had in her eighteen years of life. They turned into her small grocery store and Mary immediately busied herself behind the store counter just as the rotund derriere of the town's gossip monger wheeled in with such flounder, even the shelves could not help but be bothered.

"Josy! Josy!" The woman called for Jasmine. "Where is she?" she turned to Mary and demanded.

"Good day, Mrs. Hall," she pointed out politely that the woman had forgotten her manners. There was no return of a salutation and Mary frowned at her in dismay. "She is in the back."

Mary didn't know why the woman called Jasmine Josy. It wasn't even a logical choice for name shortening, but it was clear they had known each other for a while, so there might have been some backstory she didn't want to ask about.

"What is all the ruckus about, Jane?" Jasmine rushed out, addressing the woman. Mary rolled her eyes. She had come to find Jasmine to be quite a likable woman, but the need to gossip as much as Jane did was annoying, and every now and then she found herself missing the humming of the pots and pans at home while she washed them ready for cooking. She missed Bethany's soft voice chattering away about things in general and Joshua's insistence on bothering them both when they were having their girly moments. But even then, she didn't mind the difference in culture and people she found here, and so she paid the women no mind as they started chattering about a young doctor who worked on the Doctors Without Borders program, who had come home today to find his fiancée had off and married another man. Apparently, they had all thought he wasn't going to come home after two years away.

How cold and callous it must have been to find himself in such a fix, yet these older women were amused by what must have been his heartbreak. She sighed and tuned them out as she went about restocking the empty shelves. She stopped for a moment and hoped that her parents wouldn't just move on and think she wasn't coming back home.

"Excuse me," a soft voice interrupted her musings and she turned to look at the freckled face of Megan Jones, somewhat of an outcast in this city, having moved there for some unknown reason.

"Yes," Mary said, smiling at her. "How can I help you?"

"I am looking for honey, but I can't seem to find a bottle on your shelf." The woman who must have been her own age looked away from her. Mary had heard mean things being said about her too, but this was the second time she had been around her and she found the girl quite pleasant.

"We ran out this morning, but I am due to go collect a few bottles from the farm down the road in an hour, if you don't mind coming back."

Megan sighed and looked around at Mrs. Hall who fixed her with a disdainful eye. "No, I am okay. Thank you."

Mary watched her hurry from the store and then suffered a talking-to from the nosy woman. "Don't you be getting friendly with that girl. She is no good."

"And how do you know that?"

"People talk," Mrs. Hall said with so much determination that Mary was sure she thought that was explanation enough.

"I am not much of a fan of gossip, so I don't really care," she responded and grabbed her coat to head out after Megan. They could man the store themselves for a while.

"Hi there!" She called to the woman who was walking with sagging shoulders through the town. "Take a walk with me to pick them up."

Megan smiled and tried to decline, but Mary would not take no for an answer and so they walked in silence to the supplier just ten minutes away. Her feet ached, but she thought giving the girl some company was well worth it.

"You should boil some cerise tea for the cold you have coming on, and put some lavender oil on your pillow, by morning it should be gone."

Mary looked at her suspiciously. "That tea is as bitter as they come. I think I will pass."

Megan laughed. "Try it, you won't regret it."

They spoke about how she learnt about the powers of herbs and how she came to know so much. Mary learned that the woman had worked with a botanist for most of her life but had also been shunned from an Amish community for falling in love with an Englisch man, who later left her for an Englisch woman. With no chance of going back to her strict community, she had decided to move to this town. She made friends with an Englisch girl who later spilled her secrets to everyone and exaggerated the details, which had made it hard for her to fit in, but she was still trying.

"I figured I might as well tell you," Megan said. "You are new, but you will know soon enough."

Mary didn't know if it was the similarity of their circumstances that made her sympathetic or the fact that she really didn't understand why in a supposed liberal world as this Englisch one, Megan's story would cause such a stir. It made her even keener on holding her secret in.

"When are you due?" Megan asked, pointing at her stomach that she didn't bother hiding. It was even harder to hide it in Englisch clothes.

"In about two months, more or less." She smiled with pride.

As they spoke, she could feel a friendship blossoming, and by the time they had collected the jars of honey and made their way back to the store, lunch the following day was a plan. After two weeks she had finally made another friend, and Anna really liked her too. She wrote home to tell her mother about her that night.

"Have you thought about marriage, Mary?" Jasmine

rudely interrupted their lunch hours later with her prying comments. "You aren't getting any younger, you know. That child of yours will need a good father."

She was well aware of that fact and wanted to tell the woman as much but decided against being rude. It was not in her nature.

"I have," she responded, trying to keep her calm, "but I am young, and I am in no rush. When I do settle down, he will be perfect."

"There is no such thing," Jasmine responded without missing a beat. "Soon you will find you have ended up like me—a barren spinster."

Mary laughed at the nonchalance with which the woman stated her hopeless situation.

"Find a man soon, Mary, and make sure you have many tiny children to fill your home with laughter."

Mary had been thinking about it for a while, but considering she had just been in town, adjusting had not yet been completed and so she had not yet met any man she liked about these parts. Besides, she didn't even know what her next couple of months would be like, after the birth of her child.

More pressing things were a priority, but Jasmine and her simple mind wouldn't know that. For now, she really did need to decide how she was going to handle everything. Would she give her child away, or could she actually raise him?

Those decisions were far more pressing than her marriage prospects. Maybe it was time to look into her online job prospects so as to have more time at home to think and make these decisions.

Broken Hearts

True to her cause, Mary asked for a week off from work at the store. It wasn't her intention to go back if what Anna said about this online work would make her enough money, but she didn't want to just quit without some surety. Megan and Anna then spent the next week taking turns teaching Mary about this internet thing.

It was as fascinating as it was daunting, and when she finally got the hang of it, she went out and bought herself a huge tub of ice-cream. While eating that she felt nostalgia creeping in. It was good ice-cream. Just not as good as the homemade kind. It was in these subtle differences that Mary most found a yearning for home. She would be going on just fine, then a scent or a taste would have her aching for home. She knew more than ever, as time progressed, that living in the Englisch world was really not her calling.

After eating half the tub, she went back to the computer and found her first client on a freelance website. It was simple data entry work that took her two hours to do. The agreed price was a little more than $50 but that was two days' pay at the store. Pay she earned in less than two hours at home. At this rate she could earn a month's salary in two days and never have to get up and walk through the door.

She was sold on the idea!

When Anna got home the next day, Mary was dancing all over the house, because she had landed two more clients who paid even more than the first job. Well, her dance was really waddling, that's as much as she could do a mere 5 weeks from her due date.

"Why do you work at the office, Anna? You could be doing his!"

Anna laughed and waited until she had quieted down and then spoke. "I do work online too, but then why have one salary when I could have two?"

Mary stopped her waddling dance mid move and stared at Anna, who just laughed at her some more. She didn't feel that accomplished after all.

"You just had to burst my bubble, didn't you?"

She glared at Anna and sat back at the computer table Anna had bought her.

"If you decide to stay, you can also do the same thing."

That was a thought, but Mary knew she wouldn't. It wasn't something she wanted to talk about now though. It had her feeling like she was just breaking the hearts of the people dearest to her. The winter winds outside had nothing on the ice growing in her heart.

"How do I get this money from the computer to my pocket, though?"

"For that you need a bank account," Anna replied.

"You can use mine, but I much prefer you have your independence."

"Can we go get one tomorrow?"

Anna made a few calls to ensure she could get the day off, and close to midday when Mary finally hauled herself out of bed, both Megan and Anna accompanied her on her next step towards her Englisch life. It was a thought she instantly resented, but when the first payment came days later and she went to the ATM to learn how to withdraw it, her sense of accomplishment returned.

It all wasn't that bad. She just missed home. The baby kicked then as if on cue and agreeing with her thoughts. Then she remembered that she still had to decide what would become of his life.

Here we go again...

"What if I kept him, Anna?" she asked that night.

Anna smiled and then hugged her. "We would figure it out, but you have to tell your parents."

"I don't know if I am ready to be a parent myself. There is a lot that goes into that."

"Mary," Anna said, with a great deal of patience and care. "We keep coming back to this question, but I don't think you will know what is best for him until you know."

That reminded her of something her father used to say all the time. He would always tell her when she was younger and had issues to confront, that there is never a best situation or a worst situation. And that she really wouldn't know the best way to handle it until she knew. It had always confused her. It never made any sense and was in direct contrast to people saying she wouldn't know until she spent time figuring it out. But now seated in front of Anna, she finally understood.

She finally understood that knowing what was best for her child was not a process she could rush. She would know when she knew. Trusting in Gott, she gave it no more thought for the night. Rubbing her stomach as she worked, she decided to focus on the one thing she could affect now, and that was how much she could put in place so that, if and when she decided to keep him, it wouldn't be as hard getting by as it could be.

Happy Birthday

Three weeks later she had no choice but to face it. As she was getting ready to celebrate her nineteenth birthday, the inevitable happened.

"Mary," Megan, who had been busy in Anna's small kitchen, called to her.

She was trying to hang the Christmas lights Anna had gotten. It was the second week of December and the first snowfall had not yet christened the ground. It was as if Father Winter was waiting on something.

"Yes?" Mary answered absentmindedly. Anna had previously tried to hang these lights without help, and then gave up. Now they were a tangled mess in the box she had thrown them down in out of frustration.

"Anna, you are hereby banned from future Christmas decorating!" Mary yelled at her.

From behind the closed bathroom door, Anna was most unrepentant. "Fine. It's too much work anyway."

"Mary!" Megan all but shouted this time.

"What?" she answered, a bit annoyed but not meaning to be.

"My water broke!"

"What?" Anna poked her head out the door with her toothbrush sticking out her mouth.

Mary felt the trickling down her leg just then. "My water broke."

Her heart started beating faster than she could control. All of a sudden all the decisions she had been stalling on making came rushing back to her. In that moment she felt joy, fear and sadness all at the same time and to the same intensity. And then a feeling of hopelessness spread up her spine along with the pain of her first contraction.

Mary would recall that night as if she was just a spectator. It was the most out of body experience she had ever had. First there was the confusion to get her out of the house and to the hospital. They cleaned her up and got her into the back of a taxi just before she screamed in pain from the next set of contractions to wrack her body.

"Hold that baby in!" the taxi driver called as he swerved in and out of traffic much to Megan's chagrin.

Amidst all the madness, Anna sat beside her rubbing her back and making funny breathing sounds which Mary was supposed to imitate. She wanted nothing more than to scream at Anna that it wouldn't work, but between the pain and the crazy driving, she only had time to pray. She prayed about everything, including the salvation of whoever gave this driver a license.

When they finally arrived at the hospital, all the chaos and rush they experienced getting there was met with calm stoic faces.

"How long ago did her water break?" A nurse walked up to the screaming trio in the emergency room.

There was absolutely no haste or urgency in her voice. It was just another day at the office, while Mary screamed in pain and Anna again did that silly breathing thing. Megan answered and demanded she be given something for the pain. The nurse simply directed them to a room that smelt of antiseptic and nothing like the birthing room in her community with its lavender and rosemary scent.

"Darling," the nurse said, stopping shy of condescension. "Her water broke less than an hour ago. She has several more hours of pain before this baby is ready to come out. When she starts crowning, she will be given medicinal options to choose from."

All Mary heard was the several more hours.

"I want him out now!" she demanded.

The nurse laughed. "First time mother, right? You will soon get the hang of it."

Mary couldn't believe that was all the woman had to say. She genuinely could not believe it. Even harder to believe was that, after giving her directions on what to do while the labor pains progressed, the nurse just left with a promise to return. She was on the verge of thinking that maybe it was because she was Amish but taking a walk down the hall to ease the pain that seemed to be worse if she stood still, she realized that the rooms she passed were filled with either women going through the same or sleeping beside small new bundles of joy. She realized then why her urgency had not been returned.

"Maybe this is why my mother never had more than one child," she joked. Anna and Megan laughed.

"Maybe this is why I won't have any," Megan added.

They laughed for a few seconds before the pains started again. Mary walked, she bent, she screamed, she paused and then she prayed.

Anna had shown her pictures of childbirth online, but nothing prepared her for the pain of it. When nearly ten hours later she was rushed into a delivery room and felt her body being torn to bring life into the world, she swore she would never do it again. But when the first cries from her child reached her ears, tears of joy ran down her face. As the doctor placed him in her arms moments later and she stared down at the perfect and beautiful person she had carried for nine months, she knew she most definitely would do this again without hesitation.

"Congratulations," the doctor said, smiling at her. "You have a perfectly healthy little boy."

Mary laughed and cried at the same time. She just had no words. The baby quietened as he was placed in her arms, and she held him with such care. His eyes barely opened, and she spoke to him for the first time.

"Hi, my love," she whispered.

Beside her Anna and Megan, who had been draped and covered in sterile coats for the occasion, just looked at her and smiled.

"You did it, Mary," Anna said, resting her forehead against her. "You did it."

Mary was happy she had, but she knew better than anybody that the real hardship was about to start. Looking down at her son, a decision that had seemingly been hard to make, came easily. There was no longer a question of what she would do. Now she knew beyond a shadow of a doubt what her next step would be.

"Happy birthday, Mary," Megan said.

Laughing through her tears, Mary looked at the clock over the door. It was a few minutes after nine on December 14th. She had her best birthday gift ever, and in return she would give her son one.

The Painful Loss

Four days later she was released from the hospital. She would have gone home two days before, but as she was a first-time mother with no experienced help, the doctors thought it best to keep her a couple of days. She didn't mind, the longer they kept her the more time she would have with her son.

"Are you sure this is what you want to do?" Anna asked her as she fed the baby while Mary prepared for bed on the first night home. "This is a serious decision."

"I am sure," she replied. "I know I will not ever be able to give this child the life he deserves now, and I want him to have the best chance."

Anna looked at her as if there was something on her mind, but she didn't want to tell her.

"Out with it!" Mary demanded.

"What?"

"Anna Yoder, you couldn't keep anything from me even if you tried. So tell me what's on your mind."

Anna began with a sigh. "You said you had not

started looking for a family yet. Do you want him to be raised in the Englisch or Amish world?"

"Preferably Amish, but for that I have to find a family willing to take him in, and that will not be easy."

"It might be," Anna answered, to her surprise. "I have a cousin who lives in my community. She is married and doesn't have a child. I am sure she and her husband would take him in. That way he would be raised Amish and not with strangers we don't know. He would be family."

Mary sat up in bed. No one had told her that the exhaustion of childbirth could take this long to sleep off, but in that moment, it was forgotten.

"That's a wonderful idea! But will they take him in if they know the circumstances of his birth?"

Anna sighed yet again. "That is where the issue is. I don't think my ordnung will allow that."

"Oh," Mary said.

"But we can take him there and leave him on their doorsteps where my cousin Ruth will find him. They won't turn him away, I am sure of it!"

Mary thought about this for a while, and she fell asleep thinking about it. When she woke to change her son in the middle of the night, she was still thinking about it. She stayed home and tended to her son and worked more than usual online. She had saved more money than she ever thought possible, and she was going to make sure to give Anna some for her hospitality. The rest she intended to withdraw from the bank and leave with her son when she dropped him off.

When that would be, was something she kept delaying. She also knew Anna was right. The longer she waited, the harder it would be. Three weeks later she made the decision.

"I will take him to your cousin tomorrow," she told Anna as soon as she got in.

Anna walked over to the bassinet where her son lay sleeping. "I will miss the little guy. Did you give him a name yet?"

"I was thinking of calling him Able, but I figured it is best to leave the naming to his parents to be."

Mary said that with resolution. She didn't want to get into a conversation about all of that now. The decision she was making was life changing and it was already the hardest thing she had ever done in her life. She didn't want to make it harder, if that was even possible.

Anna took a hint and left it there. "We will take the train in the evening tomorrow, when others cannot see us entering the community. We can leave him on the porch and knock, and then wait further down the road until we see them pick him up."

Mary liked that plan. She really didn't want to just place her son on the stairs and then run off. He meant more to her than that.

The following evening that is just what they did. The early winter winds whipped around them as they walked to the train station. Mary had him swaddled against her and she pulled her coat around him to keep him extra warm. The train ride was just thirty minutes, and Anna made them get off a few miles from the community, so they could walk along a hidden path unseen. Common to both their communities was a small hidden track in the sunflower fields which bordered the main road. Now that it was winter, there weren't any flowers there to give them full cover, but the dried stalks and the dark of night did the job.

Anna carried a small basket containing the money Mary had made and a note saying she had thought to call him Able, but they could use whatever name they saw fit. The basket was padded with soft warm blankets to ward off the cold for the few minutes Able would be on the steps alone. It was a thought that broke her heart. She wanted to cry, but she was holding it all in. Tears would do her no good now.

As they walked through the fields Anna told her to stop, voices were coming their way. They stood still, dressed all in black, the night hid them well so the two teenage girls who passed them had no idea they were there. They heard them talking excitedly about what the Englisch world might be like. They were about to embark on their rumspringa journey. Mary only hoped neither of them would make the mistake she had. She was grateful for her son, but this was an isolated case of beauty coming from a horrible blunder.

"Let's go," Anna whispered as the voices faded in the distance.

They made it to the center of the community and Anna pointed to a house that looked and felt like a home, even from a distance.

"That's it," she said with a smile.

Mary held her son to her and gave him soft kisses, whispering words of love as she lowered him into the basket and wrapped him in snugly. She took the basket from Anna, and the backpack she had been carrying, which was stuffed with clothes, food and immediate necessities. Her intention was to anonymously send care packages to the house every fortnight for as long as she lived. She might be giving him up to be raised by someone else, but she was not giving him away and losing him from her memory. He was her child, and nothing would ever change that.

"Ready," she finally said to Anna, smiling down at her son as a tear slipped down her face.

Anna walked with her up to the porch and placed the bassinet on the mat in front of the door with the backpack beside it, sheltering him from the breeze. Mary bent to kiss him one more time before she made her way down the stairs to the corner post a few meters away. Anna rapped loudly on the door and then bolted down the stairs to hide beside her.

There they waited.

Sense of Duty

Ruth woke with a start. She wasn't sure what had woken her, but she was positive she had heard a loud sound. Beside her, Samuel didn't even budge. He was a deep sleeper anyway. They always joked about who would save whom if the house was ever being robbed. She sat in silence listening, but all she heard was the wind outside. Snow was late this year, but the winter winds made themselves known. When she heard no other sounds, she decided on getting herself a glass of water. If she had a child, she would have been checking in on them. The fact that she didn't made her sad.

The pail of drinking water in the kitchen was empty, it was a short walk to the outside well, and seeing that she was up she decided to brave the crisp night air to fill the pail. Bundling up, she opened the door and almost tripped head first down the stairs. The pail banged against the door as she struggled to find her footing, and Samuel called to her from upstairs.

"Ruth! Are you okay?" he asked.

"Yes," she replied. "Just tripped over something here."

"Where are you going at this hour?" he asked.

"The drinking pail is empty, and I am thirsty," she answered. "Go back to bed. I am fine."

The sound of his sturdy footsteps coming down the stairs was enough to tell her that he was going to ignore her, as usual. A baby wailing at her feet caused her to jump in fright. "What was that?" Samuel asked, coming to stand beside her.

They both looked down at where the sound was coming from and stared in surprise as their eyes made out the squealing bundle at their feet.

"It's a baby," Ruth said. She was not sure whether she was dreaming, or this was her reality, so she bent to inspect the bundle. A pair of baby blue eyes filled with tears stared up at her. She picked the little bundle up and cooed him into silence.

"Someone just left this baby here?" Samuel asked in shock. He nudged Ruth inside with him and checked the baby to see that he was okay before running barefoot down the stairs to see if he could find the person who had left the baby.

Had he walked a few more feet to the right, he would have stumbled upon Mary and Anna hiding with tearful but happy faces.

"See anyone?" Ruth called to him.

"No!" he called back over the breeze that had picked up.

Ruth turned the light on in the house as he came in and closed the door. "It's a beautiful baby boy," she said, smiling at him.

She watched Samuel closely trying to gauge all his responses. He looked just as shocked as she was.

"This bag has clothes and there is a note right here," he said, pulling it out and reading it. "It says that there is money to help get him things he might need for a while, and that they were thinking of calling him Able, but we can choose a name for him. This note is addressed directly to us, Ruth."

She smiled down at the child who was staring up at her with big baby blue eyes. Sitting at the table, she looked at her husband. "We can't just give him to the bishop then. We need to find out where he came from."

"But we can't just keep him either. You know the community will talk and the bishop will probably have a lot to say about this."

"Samuel," she began to whisper as the child's eyes fluttered closed. "This baby was given to us for a reason. It is our duty to protect him. It is clear we are not strangers to whoever left him here."

Samuel nodded in agreement, getting up to take the baby from Ruth's arms. She watched how easily he held and coddled the child, and for a moment regretted that she had not given him a child of his own.

"We will wait as long as we can and see if we can get to the bottom of this. In the meantime, you are going to have to stay here and take care of him."

She nodded and began to unpack the bag that he had brought with him, so to say. She could think of nothing else she might need, and she had enough Pampers and such to last a very long time. At least that would eliminate any suspicion to be aroused by her buying baby products. It was clear that wherever this child came from, a great amount of thought had been put into getting him to them.

Samuel kissed her forehead and pulled her to him with a smile. "Maybe this is Gott at work. Everything happens for a reason."

Ruth smiled in agreement. "We will call him Able," she said.

"Able," Samuel repeated the name as if feeling it out on his tongue. "I like it."

The only person who slept in the Beiler house that night was Able. Ruth and Samuel stayed up until dawn trying to figure out the best way to handle this development. They made plans also for how long they would wait before revealing to the bishop what had happened. They felt truly blessed and would do nothing but love and care for this child.

Outside, Mary let the tears stream down her face as she and Anna made their way back to the main road. They had waited for a while to see if Able's new parents left to report their find to the community elders, but they didn't. They had waited until they couldn't withstand the cold anymore.

"We have to go, Mary," Anna said.

Mary followed reluctantly, feeling like she was leaving the most important part of her behind. She wanted to run into the house and hold her child one more time, but she knew she couldn't, so she walked away and prayed that she had indeed made the right decision.

They made the same journey back to the city and back home, where Mary could do nothing but curl up in bed and cry. Anna watched her worriedly, but Mary assured her she would be okay. The next three weeks were nothing short of hell for her. She made sure she had more work than free time, and she turned down every invitation to go out with her two very worried friends.

At the end of the third week, she withdrew almost all the money she had and bought goods for her son, had them placed in a carton box and delivered to the Beilers. She hoped they wouldn't mind, but she would be doing that for a long time.

"Do you want to go back for him?" Anna asked her one night.

"No," she said. "I mean yes, of course I do. But that would not be the best thing for him right now. He is safe and loved where he is at. Somehow I know it."

Anna didn't push the issue anymore. "My cousin wrote to me about him. I guess she assumes I am maybe the only person she can tell. She said she hasn't told the elders yet. Do you want to see the letter?"

Mary looked up eagerly and paced the room as she read the five-page long letter. She laughed and cried as she read about all the wonderful and funny things her son was doing. She was missing it all, but Ruth seemed to really love him. The letter ended with her saying they would both do whatever it took to protect him, even leave the community if the elders did not approve.

"That won't happen, though," Anna assured her. "They are strict, but they are kind."

She held on to that with every ounce of her faith.

Finding Strength

It didn't get any easier for her though. She woke at nights, crying and missing her son. One day it finally got too much. She felt she needed some space. Not wanting to have to deal with waking in the morning and explaining to Anna why she had to go, she decided to leave immediately. She hopped on a bus just before dawn which took her in to town and, not knowing where to go, she decided to take a walk.

Mary was beginning to feel like one of those strung out women pining for a lost love, and she didn't like it. She hoped it would get better soon, but even though she knew she had made the right decision, it didn't feel any better. Anna had been right, but she would not cry. In a couple of hours it would be daylight and she was sure sleep would come a-calling but for now she was so hyped up on angry and sad energy, she had to do something.

The smart thing would have been to go get some sleep at a motel, but she knew that would be the first place her friends would check. She decided in that moment that she didn't want to see them right now at all. She felt like taking a belt to her own derriere every time she thought about having given her child up. She had been fine before that. She had been just fine, now here she was roaming about like she had no abode. In truth and in fact, she had none. She felt like she had lost her way along with her son.

An owl called somewhere close by as if mocking her moment of stupidity, and she felt a heightened sense of frustration. She needed something to take her mind off the anger she felt. She sat under the eave of a great oak tree outside an empty bus stop until the sun rose a couple of hours later, and she went to the park to see if she could find inspiration and answers on what to do next.

Entering the park, a slight breeze rustled the leaves, making them fall to the solid ground one by one. The sun had not yet begun its ascent to perform its duty of waking the tired sleepers, but she could smell the promise of morning in the air. Flowers were visible in vast quantities in the shimmering moonlight, and they concealed the freshly cut green grass now covered in dew. This park, in past days, was filled with colors, sounds and scents as visually appealing as they were relaxing. She had been instantly drawn to the energy there, and the myriad of flowers were added incentive. There were sun-collared daisies, vivid purple lilies, carrot-tinted hydrangeas, and cotton candy–pink hyacinths. The pathway was nothing more than dirt littered with random rocks drawing on nothing but natural elements for its perfection. The ground, moist from the drizzling rain the day before, caused her footing to slip just the tiniest bit, keeping her on her toes. A white picket fence ran along the trail, reminding her of the one around her Amish home that she now longed for. Despite all its natural blessing and allure, the park was barren except for her and the few early birds who tried to soothe her soul.

Walking by the small green and brown tinted pond, the milky white, soft-feathered ducks could be seen floating around, still asleep in the early hours of the morning. Soon they would be awake and battling for the scraps the passersby would throw to them. She was startled into becoming more aware of what was happening around her as an elderly couple walked by. They were dressed in their black silk slacks and cream-colored matching sweaters, and they looked at each other in amusement as if there was nothing more pleasing to them than what they saw in each other's eyes. For a moment Mary wondered if she would ever have the opportunity to grow old with someone like that. Behind the oddly shaped rocks and algae in the pond, orange, red, and yellow fish darted back and forth, drawing her attention. She couldn't see them, night vision was not among her Gott-given gifts, but she could feel their energy as they moved around in the dark… They would emerge from hiding only when the minuscule hints of bread fell, but sadly she had no such treat to offer. If you look closely enough during the day, you can see a turtle, colored forest green, blending in with the algae. It was for these reasons she enjoyed this park and its serenity.

It was the one place she had found any kind of peace in recent months.

Beyond the pond lay the lonely playground. The brick red jungle gym sat there in its solitude, longing for some eager company. In between parts of the jungle gym was the bridge to partake in children's fantasies from battling trolls to patrolling the fort. An ugly putrid brown covered it, and it was obvious that the screws were becoming unhinged. Surely it is only so long before it comes crashing down. The swings rocked gently, and the sound of the metal scraping on metal could be heard, although there was no one in sight. She would have found the place creepy if she believed in those things, but she didn't. Orange and bright in color, the swirl shaped slide echoed the belly laughs and shrill screams of children who had dared to go down the slide. Those were the sounds that could be heard in the days when you walked by and it made her wonder if she would ever live to have the chance to raise a child. To take one to the park for all these childish delights. She asked herself the question but heard nothing but silence and the stillness that echoed her life and the screams of her breaking heart. She had just given that child away.

The park offered varied scenery, which made her walk more worthwhile and effective. As the end of the path neared, her mind was refreshed, and her body was energized for the moment. She wanted to do something about the anger she felt. She had just sourced the energy to do it. Unforeseen thoughts popped into her head just as new answers for old problems unfolded, but they were still not the answers she needed.

"Where are you when I need you, Gott?" she asked in the silent morning air, hoping her voice would carry to him. No response beside a headache that seemed to be gaining in intensity by the second.

A few minutes ago it was just a throb, but now it was about to rip her head right off her body. She had been ignoring it the entire time she was walking, but her mounting frustration was not making it easy to continue ignoring it. She grabbed hold of a concrete bench on the sidewalk as the pain surged and she felt for a moment that she was going to black out. She gripped the side of her head and held the scream in, managing it just as her knees gave way.

"Mary!" She heard Anna's voice behind her. She turned to see her friend walking towards her.

"How did you find me?"

"I followed you," Anna replied. "Let's get you out of the cold."

"That won't help, Anna," she replied, her voice cracking.

"Well, let's get you back to your son."

Mary looked at her in disbelief and Anna smiled down at her. "Really?"

"Yes, maybe you should introduce yourself to my cousin and try to be a part of his life. If you miss him this much, there must be a reason for it."

Mary found strength in those words and looked forward to the possibility of it.

State your Purpose

The following day, Anna called in sick. She worried that if she dared to leave Mary alone, she would pace a hole in her living room floor, so she settled for staying home and answering all her questions as her eyes followed her left and then right.

"What if they tell the whole community and I get shunned?" Mary asked Anna.

Anna looked at her and laughed. "You can't get shunned from a community you are not a part of."

"Good point," Mary said and resumed her pacing.

She watched the clock as nervous as she was on the night that she left Able. She wondered what they would call him. Did they use her name suggestion? Or did they choose another? It didn't matter; he would always be her little Able. So many meanings could be attributed to that one name.

When the clock struck eight, they made their way to the train station and waited for the 9:00 p.m. train that sometimes came early. She knew that because this was not the first night she had sat at the train station with the intention of seeing her son. She doubted that Anna and Megan knew any of that.

"Oh, I thought I missed you guys." Megan came running up to them an hour later as they boarded. She was on night shift at the call center but had promised the two she would be there. Mary smiled at her and sat between her and Anna, clutching their hands and willing her feet to stop tapping, but for some reason the thirty-minute journey was to seem longer than usual tonight.

She had taken some pictures of Able, and she pulled the one she loved the most from her pocket and stared at it.

The driver blew his horn signaling the last boarding call and she closed her eyes and wished he would just drive already. When it pulled away minutes later, she breathed a sigh of relief. Anna got up and gave an old woman her seat and smiling with gratitude the woman took her place.

"Your son?" an elderly woman asked, who had a Bible open.

Mary smiled. "Yes."

"Your husband must be so happy," the old woman said.

Mary wondered why she would assume that when she was wearing no wedding band. But she was beginning to understand that people had these sly ways of trying to get information out of others. Either that or the woman was old and old fashioned, and so assumed she would be too. Mary decided to play along and see where it would lead.

"I don't have one of those, but maybe some time in the future I will find myself a gentleman."

"Ahh, these days it is so hard to find men of that sort," the woman lamented. "I only hope your son grows to be one."

Mary hoped so too and said as much.

"I am Freida." The old woman offered her a shaky hand encircled by a rosary. "Pleased to meet you."

"I am Mary and the same here." She smiled back. "These are my friends Anna and Megan."

"Heading off to a new life further west?" the woman asked, eyeing the backpack at her foot.

"No, just a short trip and then we come back."

"Ahh, I see," Freida said. "This train has a lot of adventurers at this hour. Plenty of fun to be had on this short trip then."

"Oh, good Gott, I hope not!" Mary exclaimed. "I am hoping for a quiet life, uneventful save for the everyday nuances of survival. Too much adventure will surely cause my death."

The older woman laughed at her proclamation. "Is it that you have had too much adventure already or are you just not interested in any more?" the woman asked.

"I have had my fair share of struggles, and I am afraid that adventures of any kind will bring more to my doorsteps." It was truly a fear she had to get over because it might kill her desire to live, but Mary had her reason. She had one year's worth of reasons and she needed not a single one more.

"Life is perspective, little one," the old woman began in a voice that bid her to listen to the wisdom she was about to impart. "And without a little adventure, we would all turn to rocks sitting in the same spot staring at the sun each day. Never let it be said that your youth is wasted on you."

Mary knew her words to be true, but as the bus went on its way, she really was hoping it would whistle her away to quiet and easy.

"I don't mind adventure, Freida," she began solemnly. "What I fear is that when the joy and spoils of adventure have passed, I will be left right where I started—and I cannot have that. I cannot be forced to start all over yet again."

The woman reached across to take her hand in her old palms, calloused with signs of working for too many years. "You should have no fear of anything life throws your way. I have a feeling you are a survivor, and with Gott by your side, be it famine or festivities you will be just fine."

She smiled, not so confident in the woman's words. She had said Gott and Mary knew then and there she was an Amish woman or had once been.

"Where is your family?" Freida asked.

"I left them to come and sort out some issues that were caused by too much rumspringa adventure."

"Ahh, you are young and Amish," Freida said, her eyes opening in joy. "So too was I once."

"Really?" Mary's attention perked up at her admission, and she waited for the woman to impart some sage advice.

"I have one piece of help to give you," Freida began, the smile leaving her face. "You make sure you enjoy life, and when you find a good man, you make him understand that you are not there just to wait on him. You state your purpose beyond that, so he will see you as a valuable addition, and once he has, you will find you can live a long and very happy life."

Mary was a bit confused, uncertain of exactly what she was speaking of, but she had a feeling she would only understand through living the reality. They spoke until it was time to disembark at their stop. As the bus drew to a halt, Freida offered a prayer on her behalf. Mary was a woman of faith and so she bowed her head in prayer too, for the life that awaited her on the outside. She could only hope it would be one she would like.

A Full Heart

"Ready?" Megan asked, rubbing her back as they stood at the edge of the sunflower fields. The night was especially cold, and Mary pulled her winter coat closer and nodded.

"As ready as I will ever be." She smiled nervously.

Anna chuckled. "That's good enough."

They retraced the steps they had taken nearly four weeks before, and with each step, Mary wondered if she would be able to see Able, and if his eyes would light up at the sight of her like they had over those three weeks. She wondered what Ruth and Samuel were like. She hoped they were all Anna had said they would be and more.

"It is so quiet here," Megan said with a hint of nostalgia. "Makes me miss home."

Mary pulled her close as they climbed the wooden stairs to the front door. "Me too."

Anna knocked with urgency and called for her cousin. The door opened just a peek moments later and Ruth's smiling face beamed at her cousin.

"Anna! Oh my! Get in here before someone sees you!"

Anna was pulled through the door and Megan and Mary quickly followed. Ruth smiled at them, but she pulled her cousin in for a long hug.

"Samuel! Anna is here!"

"What?" He hollered down the stairs. "Seems we are just breaking all sorts of rules these days."

He came running down the stairs and stopped short of hugging Anna as his eyes rested on Mary's face.

"You have Able's eyes," he said. He smiled at Anna and kissed her forehead before coming to stand in front of her.

"This is Megan and that is Mary," Anna said, pointing them out. Ruth hugged them both then she stood beside her husband and looked at Mary. She felt like she was being visually interrogated.

"She also does the same quirky thing with her eyebrows that Able does," Ruth pointed out.

Mary decided to speak. "I am overjoyed that you chose to use the name I would have given him. Yes, I am Able's mother."

A silence floated through the room as they all waited for the other to react. It was Ruth who finally spoke moments later as she took a seat. Samuel poured her a glass of water from the drinking pail she had been carrying the night she found Able.

"Are you here to take him back?" Ruth asked her.

Mary looked at her in shock. "Only if you don't want him."

"Oh no!" Ruth got up from the table to hug her. "We love the little guy, and my heart would break if he ever had to go, but no more than your heart must have been breaking to leave him here. What happened?"

Mary looked at Anna and Megan, who smiled and encouraged her to tell them. For the next twenty minutes, she told them everything from start to finish. When she was done, both Samuel and Ruth were staring at her in shock.

"You were outside that night?" Samuel asked.

Anna laughed. "You came so close to us, Sam."

They all chuckled and the mood in the room lightened.

"Would you like to see him?" Ruth asked her.

"Oh, very much," Mary said. "But I don't want to wake him."

"Oh, he is not asleep," Samuel laughed. "Sleeping is not his favorite thing to do at all."

Mary stood at the bottom of the stairs as Samuel brought Able down. The baby smiled as he was placed in Mary's arms. Her heart felt full at the sight of him.

"He looks so happy," she said through her tears.

"Well, you did send him to us to love him and take care of him, and that is exactly what we intend to do."

Mary kissed her son, who cooed. Anna pulled her new phone from her pocket and took pictures.

"If you want to be a part of his life, Mary, we welcome that. We understand your circumstances and we are happy you chose us, but that doesn't mean your son can't grow to know you."

"Really? I would love that!"

They sat in silence as Mary just stared at his beautiful face. All the broken pieces of her heart mended themselves as she sat there smiling down at her son.

"We would like to adopt him as soon as possible, if you are sure of this," Samuel said a bit hesitantly.

Mary could sense that he really didn't want to broach this topic with her but did so out of necessity.

"I was thinking that was the most logical thing to do. I don't want him growing up as an outcast. An adoption would free him from all the stigma my mistake would bring to his life. What did your community elders say?"

Ruth and Samuel looked at each other and Mary knew that meant they had not told them just yet.

"We will first thing tomorrow, and while they might frown at the situation, I know they will not object."

Mary didn't want to have to wonder about any of that. "Well, tell them tomorrow and then we will come back here in two days and see. In the meantime, I will look into the adoption papers."

Anna cleared her throat. "I hope neither of you think I am too forward, but I did a little of that research already. I spoke to lawyers, who gave me the documents you and Mary will have to go through and sign."

Mary smiled with gratitude as Anna placed the papers on the table. "I will go through these tomorrow with Ruth," Samuel said as the baby yawned. Mary reluctantly handed him over to be put to bed.

"You need to tell your parents, Mary," Ruth said. "Don't wait too long and don't make them find out from anybody else."

She knew they were right. That was the next step on this journey. She decided that would be her first stop the next time she came this way. That next time would be in two days. Two hours later, Ruth packed them up with a basket of baked goods and fresh vegetables and sent them on their way.

"Thank you so much." Mary turned to them and smiled. "Thank you for being willing to take him in."

"You are more than welcome," Samuel said, and his warm smile creased his cheeks.

When Mary left, her earlier sadness was gone. She hugged Anna and Megan and laughed. She really could not express how grateful she was to them.

The Confrontation

It was another month before Mary found the courage to confront her parents. This time she decided she would do it alone. Winter had finally decided to come to their quaint little town, and the streets were covered in layers of white heavenly powder. Anna hugged her as she made her way to the train station and handed her a phone.

"Call me when you get there so I know you are safe and call me if you need me to get a taxi and come get you," she demanded.

Mary was hoping if she did have to call Anna, it wouldn't be because after hearing the news her parents had kicked her out of their house. She was hoping beyond words that was not going to be the outcome. She took the same bus she had before. This time she rode it past four more stops and for a further thirty minutes. She closed her eyes most of the way and thought about how happy she would be if her parents would accept her and her son. She knew that going there and asking that of them might be too much, but she was still going to try.

When she got off the bus, it was minutes before ten and a familiar buggy was coming up the road; she wanted to hide, but the fact that the horse was nudged into a steady trot meant he had seen her.

"Mary Lapp, is that you?" Amos called around the balaclava that was protecting his nose from the biting winter air.

He stopped his buggy beside her and hopped down. All she could manage was a simple hello.

"Oh, don't look so mortified," Amos laughed at her. "I am not one to judge you. There has been a lot of gossip, but I like to give people the opportunity to explain themselves, though you most certainly do not need to explain to me. It is just nice to see you."

She sighed. "Nice to see you, too," she admitted, blushing as he tucked a strand of her hair back under the cap she had worn to keep her head warm. His touch was electrifying and just then she was reminded that she had always liked Amos. Something about him had always pulled her in and intrigued her, but rumspringa had got in the way, and then everything else.

"You coming back home, or just going to visit your parents?" he asked.

"I am not sure which just yet," she replied.

He chuckled. "I completely understand that. Let me give you a lift. It's really cold tonight."

She graciously accepted and he helped her into the surprising warmth of the buggy.

"Can we just sit here for a minute, please?" she asked him, grabbing on to his hand before she realized it.

He smiled and sat across from her, covering her hand with his. "Whatever it is, your parents will understand. I just think they miss you more than you could even imagine."

She knew they might, but she wasn't sure it would be as simple as that. After a few minutes she told him she was ready to go. He stopped the buggy at her gate and helped her down. Walking her up the porch, he hugged her.

"I hope to see a lot more of you around here, Mary Lapp. Yours is a face I miss seeing, even if it is in passing. Maybe we could have lunch sometime?"

Mary wasn't sure if he was inviting her out on a date, and she was even less sure he would want to date her. Amos came from a traditional, non-deviant Amish family. His grandfather was an elder and his father was training to be a bishop. Getting involved with her was likely not something they would approve of. She pushed the thought aside though and knocked on her parents' door. When it was eased opened a few moments later, her father's face creased into a huge smile.

"Mary is home!" he called over his shoulders and pulled her in from the cold and into the warm embrace she had missed so much.

Her mother came quickly from around the corner and it was as if she had just left that day. The hugs and kisses never ended, and her mother tried to feed her as soon as she sat at the table.

"This house has been way too quiet without you and your noisy friends," her mother said with a smile. "Are you home to stay?"

"Well, that rather depends on you and Daed," Mary

admitted. "I am ready to tell you why I left, and then you can decide what will happen next."

Her mother placed three cups of hot chocolate on the table and sat down. "Go ahead, Dochder."

"I was pregnant with an Englisch man," she began. The sharp inhalations from her parents made her cringe, but when her mother spoke, nothing but tears streamed down her face.

"So where is my grandchild, Mary? Why are you here alone?"

Mary took both parents' hands in hers and took her time explaining all that had transpired since she left for rumspringa.

"How far away do these Beilers live?" her father asked. "You say they are Anna's relatives?"

"Yes, and they live one town over."

"I want to meet my grandchild and we can figure out what to do from there," her father said matter-of-factly. She expected her parents to lament her mistake and make her promise to confess and join the church, yet here they were, more concerned for their grand-child. They chatted for another hour and then her mother rushed her off to bed, saying in the morning they would go to visit Able.

She got very little sleep, and when she made her way downstairs for breakfast like it was a normal day, her parents were already dressed to go. Within the hour they were being introduced to Ruth, Samuel and Able, who instantly took to his grandfather.

"The adoption is almost finalized, and the commu-nity here has accepted him, but whenever you want to spend time with him, that is fine by us," Ruth assured them. Mary watched her mother swoon over Able and all was beginning to feel right in the world again.

She remained at home during the following months, going through her training and confession to be fully accepted into the church. Amos was the first person to step up to her when she had completed all that was required for her to be accepted into the faith.

"So how about I make us some lunch tomorrow and you meet me by the creek?"

She laughed and was about to turn him down, but he was not taking no for an answer. Her confession had excluded the details about her son, because she had agreed with her parents to keep that quiet for now, but the elders knew and soon Amos would too. She decided if he wanted to be a part of her life, that was something he had to prove he could accept.

The following day met her with the usual nervousness, but when she sat beside Amos and told him about it all he turned to her and smiled. "If he is as lovely as his mother, he will break many hearts."

Mary laughed and Amos placed a hand over hers.

"We all make mistakes, Mary," he said, dipping his toes into the running water of the cold creek. "It is not our mistakes that define us; it is what we make of them. Besides, who was to say this wasn't Gott's plan for your life all along?"

She squeezed his hand and smiled. "Do you want to meet him?"

"Right now, if you have the time," he said excitedly, and so they made their way to Ruth and Samuel, ignoring the fact that they both had work to do. On the way out, her mother called to her to tell her there was a letter from Anna. She hopped from Amos's buggy to get it. When she opened it, she smiled. It was a wedding invitation for early spring. Anna was finally taking the plunge with the Englisch boy she had fallen in love with.

All was indeed right in the world.

Amos smiled at her as they were heading out. For the first time in a very long time, she was truly happy.

The Marriage

Eighteen months later

Anna and Evan had finally taken the plunge and were married at his parents' expansive home in the hills. The wedding had been a grand and wondrous affair with more people than Mary knew, but now she just wanted to be alone with her family—Anna and Evan included. Able, who was now running and climbing, had kept her busy for most of the day, while Ruth went crazy in the kitchen and Samuel made friends easily while doing the work Ruth laid out for him.

Now she was all alone with Anna and Megan, who was there to attend a wedding with her gentleman friend, Ryan, who Mary thought was wonderful. He was a US Marshal and she was beginning to wonder if Gott was putting these men in their lives to keep them on the straight and narrow. Maybe they would have another wedding soon, or so she was hoping. She looked behind her to where Amos stood trying desperately to figure out some ornament Evan's mother had told him to pack away. It was not going so well at all.

Mary sipped on the glass of wine Anna had poured her as they looked out at the men on the patio trying to figure out how to work the new grilling oven they had spent all morning building from Evan's fantastical idea. They placed the charcoal on stone across which they placed a piece of mesh wire, propped up by two stones. The men looked at it in awe as if it were the greatest invention of all time.

"Do you think we should go help them?" Megan asked as they laughed at the utter masculine hopelessness before them.

Mary was out of that lot. She was down for frying eggs, making toast and coffee; these days, anything else might prove a bit of a challenge. That was the excuse she had given Amos over the last few days. He was a master chef, and she intended to string him with an apron every chance she got, even if that meant playing the poor helpless damsel. She looked at Ryan, who shoved the other men away and got the grill started in under a minute.

"We have a winner," she said, looking at Megan, who gazed at her man with nothing but pride. She wondered if that was what she looked like even now, looking at Amos. He turned as if he had sensed her staring at him through the open door, and catching her eye, he winked. She thought that he was a man she would certainly learn to cook for.

As Evan flexed his shoulder, the smile on Mary's face dulled just the slightest. She wished she could have them all in one place, but Anna was now fully immersed in the Englisch world. Megan had long since made her peace with the same, and she loved her home too much to stay. She would settle for the biweekly visits that she never missed. They would all come by Mary's for an early supper, before they would pile into her father's buggy and go on the ride to visit Able. Some days Ruth and Samuel came to them. Mary saw her son no less than four days every week, and she looked forward to the visits more and more each time.

"You get used to it," Megan said, rubbing her back. "You get used to it, but you never stop worrying and wanting it all, but this is as close to perfection as our traditional ways will get. We will make it work."

Megan followed Mary's gaze to where the men had just placed the steaks onto the grill. They stood around it, guarding…she wasn't so sure what they were guarding, or if they thought the intense stares would make it cook any quicker.

"I still worry every day about losing this much happiness, but we only lose what we take for granted. After a while when it keeps showing up, and you just stop thinking about it. You will worry, but you won't let it consume you." Megan said and Anna pitched in.

"The big advantage you have is that you have lived that life too, Mary," Anna said. She smiled at the women who had become her sisters. The ones who had been there for her when she most needed the support. Anna was like an unpredictable sister, who always had a look of mischief in her eyes. Megan was the older, more stoic sister who tried to keep them all in order with kind advice and soft wisdom.

They had never left her much over the years and she had grown to love them for what they brought to her life.

"Come on," Megan urged and took up the bowl of vegetables to head outside. Anna followed with the macaroni pie and Mary downed the rest of her wine in one go and headed after them.

"I told you that you need to put oil or something of the sort on the thing or it will stick to the grill," Ryan said, studying a recipe book they had found.

"This is not a toy, you buffoons," Evan's mom said and took the basting brush from Evan who was too busy glaring at the others to follow Ryan's instructions. She basted the steak and turned it over, exposing the char.

"That one's yours, Amos," Evan said, laughing.

"You burn it and I eat it? Not going to happen."

Evan turned and waved a piece of meat at him. "I am the groom today, so my wish shall be your command."

"Here we go," Megan laughed. They had spent days listening to the men banter about their positions now that Evan was the first to be getting married, with Ryan playing referee occasionally.

Ryan intervened just before Amos and Evan would have started sword fighting with their forks and she watched the children in them come out to play.

"Are you ready for the fight of your life?" Amos asked and a sorrowful shadow fell over Evan's face.

"Anna will always come to my rescue," Evan said, sounding more like he was trying to convince himself.

Anna laughed and brought her glass to her lips.

"Sure, my love. Always." The sarcasm only made Evan look like she had taken his favorite toy away.

"Tell me when was the last time you had to defend

your honor?" Amos chided, enjoying his moment. "Soon I will lead you to your demise!" he said as they fought on as if their forks were swords, until Evan's mother smacked them upside the head again on her way out.

Anna went to hug Evan, glaring at Amos who was trying hard to contain his joy. Ryan slapped him across the head which didn't help at all and he laughed as he made his way to Mary.

The usual routine for Englisch weddings was that the bride and groom would ride off into the sunset for a wonderful honeymoon, but Anna and Evan had decided they would spend it with the people who meant the most to them. Mary looked around the table after all the guests had gone. Ruth and Samuel looked right at home. Her own parents were making their way up the stairs and Anna and Megan looked happy. Beside her, a tired Able, who had eaten more sweets than she liked and played more than he could manage, was asleep in the bassinet. Beside her, Amos laced his fingers with hers and brought her hand to his lips before saying the grace. And then dinner carried on with much the same banter, and hours later, as the others turned in for the night, Mary pulled him onto the couch. She had been dying to have him to herself all day.

They sat there without the need for words and she enjoyed his hand in hers.

"I love you," he whispered, and she smiled, for no words would ever be enough to tell him how much she loved him too. He was a man who had looked at her brokenness and loved her until all her pieces fit just right. He was her second greatest gift ever. She gave thanks for him every day. And if that day should come, she would happily wed the man who had stepped up and supported her when everybody else in the community had been undecided.

Gott worked in amazing ways. From her horrible mistake, nothing but an abundance of beauty and joy had been found.

Rainfall and Smiles

Mary sat looking out at the rain and smiling. She was in a very somber mood, but the rain always had a way of making her feel like all was right with the world. She was drinking a hot cup of green tea and praying she didn't get the chills, having been soaked on her way back from seeing her little bundle of joy. Not even the rain was going to stop her weekly visits.

"You okay?" Megan came out to ask her, coming up behind her and rubbing her shoulders.

She smiled at her best friend and nodded. There was a lot she would say about how she was feeling at the moment, but she wasn't going to give in to that urge. She wanted neither Anna nor Megan thinking she was at all envious of them. She wouldn't allow that. Anna had been her closest friend since falling pregnant by an Englisch boy while on rumspringa. She had met Megan after escaping to the Englisch world to live with Anna after her pregnancy belly had started to show; Megan was like the stable and not so crazy older sister she had always wanted. Together, they had figured it all out.

Mary would have to admit that they had carried most of the burden of figuring out things for her, and she did not now want them feeling guilty.

Anna and her husband Evan had been blessed with a beautiful baby girl two months before, and Megan was now carrying a child of her own. Mary and her husband Amos had been battling for five years to conceive, but it simply was not happening. She was beginning to wonder if maybe Gott was punishing her for having Able out of wedlock. Her sweet little five-year-old Able was more of a blessing than she could ever have hoped for.

Again, she felt happiness flooding through her. She had given Able up for adoption two months after his birth, which was the hardest decision she had ever had to make. Up to that point, deciding on rumspringa and leaving home was her biggest stress. Looking at her infant son back then, she knew that giving him up would be the best for him at the time, but it was the most difficult decision of her life. She had been unable to function effectively for months after abandoning him to the loving family she had chosen, who were members of Anna's family who had not yet been blessed with their own boppli. Giving the boppli to someone within her own Amish community to raise had made the decision easier. It had been difficult leaving Able on the doorstep that winter night, with Anna by her side, but it had also been the best decision she had made for her son.

At the time she had no idea how anyone would have reacted, and she did not want her son to grow up ostracized by the community in which she had grown up and which she had loved for so long. When the pain of losing him hadn't diminished with time, she decided it was time Anna's cousin, Ruth, and her husband Samuel were introduced to the person who had brought that boppli to them that night. Their reaction had been better than she would ever have expected. When she eventually confessed all to her parents, they had also supported her wholeheartedly. Amos had been the first in the Amish community to accept her back in the fold, and was now her husband whom she loved dearly, but they had not been able to conceive a boppli of their own. Mary was well aware that the responsibility was not her own but somehow she felt Gott was punishing her for the sins of her rumspringa. She felt penance was required, but even so the blessing of a boppli had not presented.

It had been five years, five very long years, and she desperately wanted that to change. But for now, she would be happy for her friends, Anna and Megan, who were happily married and raising kinner.

"You seem a bit distant today," Megan said, pulling her from her thoughts. "Is everything okay?"

Unable to risk speaking out loud, she simply reached across the table, took her friend's hand and smiled. She hoped that would be enough to convince Megan that she was indeed okay although that was somewhat of a lie.

"Hi, Mary!" little Michael called to her as he ran by in the rain. Amos called him her doting admirer. Since her return, he spent time with her after school and between chores. He was a curious one who always brought a smile to her face. He was also good with Able, and she suspected a little lonely as he was an only child, so she welcomed his company.

That night she spoke to Amos when he got home about her concerns. As usual he assured her that all was fine and everything would be just as they wanted, all in Gott's time. Had this been five years before, she would have no problem accepting Gott's time frame, but with everything that had happened in her life, she knew that, all things considered, he was right. It was with a heavy heart that she turned in that night, hoping to be with child before the year end, and that they could finally move on as a happier family. Until then, she would give Able all the love she had in the hopes that he knew that her love for him would not change if she had another child.

The Silent Prayer

The sound of death rang out around Ellen, and she could feel the chords of it suffocating her. No matter how she tried, she just couldn't get away from it. It was everywhere! She walked into the bedroom she had shared with her husband for so many years, and she could almost feel his presence, but he just wasn't there. She could smell the Brut aftershave he sometimes used. It would burn her nose, and when she complained, he would kiss her on the tip of her nose. She walked down the stairs of the house they had made a home and expected to see him in the kitchen shuffling about in the cupboard for a quick snack before going out to the fields, but all that was left was the ghost of his memory. Nothing was visually there to hold her sight and bring a smile to her face.

He was gone…

A fact she was having a hard time adjusting to. Even repeating those words out loud did nothing to soothe her aching soul. He had died the day before after battling cancer for two years. A part of her resented the fact that they could have probably been helped sooner by Englisch doctors. At first his sickness and weakening were passed off as a tenacious cold by the community doctor. He had said that it would get better. After a year, she had asked the bishop to let them consult a specialist. By then it was far too late. His prostate cancer had already progressed to stage four, and a change of diet had just not been enough to right him. He had become a shell of himself and she had seen the life slowly leave him months before he actually died. Now that he was gone, she was not as prepared as she had anticipated she would be.

"Ellen." She heard the soft call from her doorway and knew that Ruth would not go away unless she answered.

She was in no mood for a friend, but Ruth Beiler had been there for her for most of her life, and she would respect that friendship even in this time of grief. She walked to the door and silently let her in, opening the door and walking away. With Ruth there was no need for words right now, but she knew they would come.

"I am sorry, Ellen," Ruth said, squeezing her hand supportively.

Ellen still had no words. She sat silently at the kitchen table in her nightgown and Ruth made her a cup of tea and a sandwich. She instantly thought how much harder it would be to live now. Ellen and her late husband had never been able to have kinner, and their request to see an Englisch specialist on the matter of conceiving years before had been denied by the bishop.

"Gott has a plan for your life, and it is not for us to question it," the bishop had said.

Now here she was without a child or a husband, and

she felt lonely. Even in the presence of a friend, she felt lonely. And the twinge of another unfamiliar emotion started to creep in. Ruth placed the food before her and she willed herself to take a bite of the sandwich which was no doubt made with love, sympathy and just a pinch of pity. That thought irked Ellen slightly. She didn't want Ruth's pity.

Ruth had Able now, and Samuel was still alive while she had nothing and no one. Gott had seen it fit to bless Ruth with Able, Mary Lapp's child, but he had not seen it fit to bless Ellen with a boppli even though neither of them had been able to conceive. For five years she had watched Ruth nurse and love the child that had shown up on her doorstep, and she had waited and prayed for her own miracle; but Gott took the one human being she had left in the whole world instead.

She could feel the anger creeping in, but she tried to contain it.

"Will you be making arrangements?" Ruth asked.

Ellen tried to control the anger rising in her. "He just died, Ruth. I am in no state of mind to be getting out of bed, much less making arrangements."

She realized how harsh her words had been by the look of shock that flashed across Ruth's face. Ever the faithful and understanding friend, the other woman just reached across the table and squeezed her hand.

"I know, Ellen," Ruth whispered. "If you would like, I can go ahead and handle it for you."

To let someone else handle her husband's passing felt like somewhat of a betrayal, so Ellen shook her head.

"It's okay, and I'm sorry for snapping at you."

Ruth smiled again. "It's okay. Under the circumstances, I can understand."

Ellen sighed. She needed to have her husband's body prepared for the viewing before the service and his burial, but she really could not step foot outside today.

"I appreciate the help," she replied. "Can you have them get him ready for the viewing? It will be tomorrow and then his burial."

Ruth nodded and asked what clothing she wanted him dressed in, to which Ellen answered in an absent-minded way. She told Ruth where to find the clothes and then showed her out the door. The door closed after her and Ellen broke down and cried, thinking about the lonely little burial site on the hill not too far from the forest. It was filled with wooden crosses marking grave sites. Wooden crosses that would rot over time leaving only rocks to mark the eternal resting place of her love.

The fact that she was childless came back to her mind and she cried even more. Had she been blessed with a child to remember her husband by, losing him might have been easier to bear. But no such luck. She thought of Ruth and Able. How the child's laughter and even tears had filled the Beiler house with life over the last five years. Ruth had changed. She had a glow which only mothers somehow had. Samuel was always a happy man. Even when Ruth had been worried they would never have a child, Samuel, her husband, had always seemed to be glowing with a radiant joy that came solely from the fact that he was alive. She had thought that he could not possibly glow any more without spontaneously combusting. Samuel's glow took on a whole new light after Able arrived, the son they were gifted with while she and her husband could only look on with love, support and hope for them.

When her husband had fallen ill, he had said that he might be the reason for them not having a boppli. By then it didn't matter; she had just wanted him to be healthy so that they could be happy again. She had never considered that she might be burying him so soon. She felt as if her life was over. Mentally, she was drained and just uncertain of everything now happening around her.

"Ellen!" She heard calls from outside, recognizing the voice as the youngest serving elder, Ahab Declus. She was in no mood for him or the throng of well-wishers and sympathizers she spotted outside her home, bearing food. She sat quietly in the living room and ignored their calls, wishing them away. A few minutes later, she heard the bishop directing them to leave their basket of goodies on the porch and give her some space. She breathed a sigh of relief as she felt the tears coming again.

She wasn't sure if she was crying because she was angry or because she had just resigned herself to her fate. Childless or husbandless? Somehow, she felt the answer to that question did not quite matter anymore. She simply cried.

She stared at an empty space all day. It was not until dusk that she willed herself to take up the food that had been left for her. She nibbled absentmindedly, less out of the want for food and more out of need. Taking a long soak in the tub her husband had built her, she eventually turned in for the night, hoping she would be able to get up the next day. If she couldn't, she hoped the community would understand and just leave her alone.

That night, she fell asleep with a prayer on her lips and a song of sadness in her heart. He really wasn't coming back. Her husband was gone to a better place, where she hoped to see him again someday, but for now she knew, despite the grief, life would go on. She had to go on.

Ellen had no clue what tomorrow would bring, but she decided she wouldn't let it force her to remain in this depressing place. She would handle this blow and try her best to move on. He would want her to.

The Gift from Gott

"Hi," Amos whispered, hugging her from behind. Mary closed her eyes and leaned back into the embrace.

On most days, all she needed was the feel of his arms around her. As always, the thought of being childless was on her mind, but today she would push it aside. They were going to be working on the small garden patch to the side of the house, where she had always wanted to grow peppers and cherry tomatoes. Megan had called the small vegetables a niche market in the community. More often than not. Once could only come by this produce biweekly at the farmers market in town, which could be inconvenient.

"Do you want the planting plot plowed out closer to the back or the side of the house?" Amos called back to her.

She thought for a minute. "To the side! Better sunlight there."

She wondered for a moment whether these plants needed more sunlight and shrugged. If they did, she could always replant the area with grass and move the plot closer to the back. Losing herself in the thought of what it would be like, the knock on the door drew her out of her daydreaming.

"Amos! I brought the seeds!"

Mary smiled and ran to the front door, to find Evan. Evan was Anna's husband, whom she rarely got to see him because he was Englisch, but here he was grinning at her.

"The gorgeous Mary Lapp. As beautiful as the day I met her."

Mary giggled and blushed as she hugged him. "You had better stop or I will call Anna and tell her you are up here flirting with women."

"Oh, not women, Mary Lapp," he joked. "Just you."

"If you don't stop trying to steal my woman whenever you come here, Anna and I are going to have to figure out an appropriate punishment."

Amos stood behind her with a big grin and laughed as he embraced Evan like the best friends they had quickly become. It had not always been this smooth. The dutiful Amos had found Evan's Englisch ways somewhat hard to accept, but after five years that was no longer a problem. They chatted before excusing themselves and, with the thunder rumbling in the distance, they got to work on preparing the small garden for planting.

She could hear them joking around and listened to the joy in Evan's voice as he spoke about his growing daughter, Mary-Ann. It was with pride that Mary had accepted the significance of her name.

"And Mary?" Evan asked.

After a pause, she heard Amos answer. "Still not

pregnant and worried Gott might be punishing her because of how Able was conceived."

Evan inhaled sharply with shock. "She can't possibly believe that!"

"Yes, she does and no matter how much I try to reassure her that's not the case, she isn't taking it so easily."

Silence fell and Mary knew she should walk off then and leave the men to their privacy, but she felt compelled to stay.

"Have you considered going into the town to see a specialist?" Evan asked.

"I suggested that, but you know we would have to get permission. I am not so sure the elders would allow it."

Evan chuckled. "I think Mary is a prime example that elders might allow many things within reason. She is back here and so is Able, and you two are married and happy. Many of those things would have been considered impossible before."

The sound of the garden shovels stopped. "Very true," Amos replied.

"I think sometimes both the Amish and the Englisch forget some very important things," Evan said, and Mary could hear the deep thinking in his voice.

"What do you mean?" a curious Amos asked.

"Well, Gott created both worlds. The Amish sometimes forget that Englisch medicine is a gift from Gott too, but I can respect your beliefs. What the Englisch fail to understand is respect and appreciation for the simpler things in life, and we sometimes pay a price for that. My point is, having married an Amish woman, I see sometimes where these worlds could both benefit from the other. You and Mary might need our help. I say don't hesitate to ask for it. You never know what that might lead to."

Mary left them to get on with her own chores, while thinking about the possibilities. She could still hear murmurs from the men but could no longer eavesdrop. Consulting a specialist might help. She would be open to that suggestion if the elders and the bishop would allow it. If Amos did in fact suggest that at the end of the day, she would not hesitate to say yes. If he didn't, she would come up with a way to bring it up.

Evan left them just before nightfall, and the rain that had been gracious enough to wait until then released showers of blessings an hour later. She hoped he was safely back home with Anna before the rain started, as he should have been since home was only thirty minutes from them. That night in bed, Amos pulled her close and whispered in her ear.

"You know I am not bothered that we do not have a child yet, right?"

The use of the word "yet" did not soothe her. In fact, it made her more anxious about whether or not she would be able to carry a child.

"I know, but it bothers me."

He hugged her tighter. "I know it does. Evan was telling me that he and Anna saw a specialist just before her pregnancy. Nothing was wrong with Anna, they just wanted to make sure her body was ready to carry a child. He told me about some fertility medicines she was given, and he reminded me that the problem could also be with me. So I am wondering if you want us to ask permission to visit a specialist."

She smiled in the darkness. "Do you think they will let us?"

Amos sighed. "They could decide it's no problem, or they could say they have already made enough allowances for us. We will never know unless we try."

She nodded and agreed that they would see the bishop come morning. They lamented the death of Ellen's husband before falling asleep, with a promise that they would spend many more years together.

With daybreak the following day, they accompanied Ruth to deliver flowers to Ellen. She refused to answer her door.

"I am worried about her," Ruth said with a frown.

Mary sighed. "I think, under the circumstances, she is allowed to be a recluse."

They left with heavy hearts that were immediately lightened at the sight of Able dancing around Ruth's backyard with the chickens he was meant to be tending. Mary couldn't help but smile. He was perfection. An epitome of joy and an abundance of laughter. Though he was barely accomplishing what he was assigned to do, he was having so much fun, and so they didn't bother him. She hoped she would be able to give him a sibling very soon. They left him to his playing and Mary made her way with Amos to the bishop's house.

The conversation there was brief. They got a Yes with a warning not to make this a habit, and though she disliked the inference, she was happy for their permission. Without hesitation, they piled into their buggy and headed to the address Evan had given them the day before.

The office was small and personal. Three women

were already seated in the waiting room and, as expected, they stared without reservation when the Amish couple entered. Mary was not bothered by it all, but Amos was a little less comfortable. Luckily they did not have to wait long. After speaking to the receptionist and explaining why they were there and who had referred them, they were ushered into a fancy room to wait. Surrounded by machines on a single bed in the middle of the room, the examination made Mary a little uncomfortable, and after Amos was checked, they left with a prescription for vitamins. The pharmacy alongside was pricier than they were used to, but she didn't fuss.

With renewed hope, they went back to Ruth's to play with Able before returning home with high expectations. That night she prayed that it would all work out for the best. She would trust in Gott. He and He alone knew what was best.

Gone to Heaven

It was a month before Ellen found the courage to step outside her house. Two days after that, death gripped the community again and she could not help but wonder if this was a sign from Gott. Usually she would be caught up talking about it with Ruth, but she found the need to avoid the other woman. She wasn't ready yet for the joy and radiance of the Beiler household. She wasn't even ready to hear from people at all, so she just kept to herself mostly. On days like today, she helped out at the schoolhouse. Ellen now stood by the door watching the crowd grow. As news of Emily's death spread, the community came to stand in solidarity. Emily had become quite the sensation when she had taken over the schoolhouse and taken in her younger sister's child. Theirs was quite the story.

"Ellen." She looked down at the little boy tugging on the hem of her blue frock.

"Yes, Jake," she said to the four-year-old whose big gray eyes swam with tears.

"Why is everybody crying for my Aunt Emily?"

She sighed, guessing he had indeed been too young to be educated about death. The ordnung prepared each Amish person to meet their maker, but that was a philosophy even a four-year-old could not really be expected to grasp.

"Remember I told you that your mamm had gone to heaven to be with the Lord?"

"Yes," he said, wiping at his nose. "That's why I will never see her again."

"Well, that's the same thing that has happened to your Auntie Emily," she said slowly. He looked up at her, his bottom lip quivering beneath the weight of trying to keep in those unshed tears.

"But we were to go to the river today," he said, and a tear slipped down his face. "Was it something I did wrong, why she left?"

Ellen tried to hold back her own tears. How was she going to explain to a four-year-old that his father had abandoned him for an Englisch woman and her world, and that his mother had likely died of heartbreak, and now his loving aunt, who had taken him in as her own, was dead too? How was she expected to tell him that the reality of life was that they all lived to die at some point?

"No, Jake," she began, bending to his level as the mourners made two waves around them, not caring to look down at them as they made their way to Emily's bedside where songs of eternal rest were being sung. She picked him up and walked out of the house, heading for the large almond tree to the left of the property. They could hear the sounds of the spring close by, strengthened by the late summer rains that had been falling. When she set him down in the morning shade and took a seat beside him, he instantly huddled into her and stared with fear at the people entering the house they had just left.

"Who will take care of me now?" he asked, and another tear slipped down his face. She had always found him to be a smart little boy and he had endured many hardships of Amish life in his young life. She had once heard children teasing him about his father running out on him.

"Shush, little one," she whispered, pulling him closer to her. Truth be told, she had no idea who would be taking care of him. From their silent perch beneath the great almond tree, they watched people come and go and the chorus of goodbyes rise and fall. All sounds stopped abruptly as Jonathan and Harry made their way to the house, the community leader entering dressed in his blue shirt. She sat wondering if not for any reason but the death of his teacher, he couldn't have donned the traditional clothing. Jonathan had just been made one of the elders of the community. At fifty-one he was still considered to be very young.

Ellen never had a problem with him, but she stayed out of his way, mostly because she didn't know how to feel about the man. He had changed since the times when they had grown up together as children. The jovial young man who was rarely away from his beloved horses had all but disappeared. She hated to think that power had changed him, but the absence of another explanation made thinking otherwise almost impossible.

Minutes after entering, he again exited the house, stopping on the porch to look around as if he had misplaced something. When he saw her across the way, he headed in her direction. Looking down at little Jake, she realized that he had fallen asleep in her arms; not wanting to wake him, she sat still and waited for the man to reach her. His powerful strides closed the gap between them easily.

"Sister Ellen," he said softly, smiling down at her. "How are you?"

"Under the circumstances," she said, casting him a knowing glance.

"Yes, terrible news, isn't it?" he said, and she braced herself for what was still to come. "We understand that little Jake here has nobody to care for him just now. We were wondering if you could keep him for a few days while we made other arrangements."

She looked up at him in shock. She had expected something, but such a grand favor was a surprise to her. Could she decline? She could, she was well aware of his propensity for allowing choice, but glancing down at the sleeping boy, she just knew she wouldn't say no.

"Yes, no problem," she answered. After all she had well passed the age where suitors were lined up at her door begging her to court them. The one man, beside her late husband, she loved had decided to leave to be a doctor in the Englisch world. Jonathan had yet to marry. She was thinking that a man of his stature would have had Amish women lining up to be with him, but that wasn't the case.

"Thank you, Ellen," he said before excusing himself. "Harry here will ensure you have all you need for the time he will be with you."

She nodded her gratitude and exhaled as he walked away. Here was her chance to be a parent. She knew it was rumored that Jake had family in the Amish community a few towns over, she hoped that was not the arrangement Jonathan had referred to. She brushed the thought aside and made her way home to see to her young charge.

That joy would not last very long though, because three weeks later, just as she was getting used to the house being messy, Jonathan came calling.

"We are here for Jake," he said, handing her a thank-you basket of fresh products. "His grandmother was found."

Ellen felt her heart break all over again. She wanted to scream that they could not have him. She wanted to scream that they had been evil for allowing her to settle into the rhythm of caring for him, but she couldn't. She stepped out of the doorway to allow them inside. Jake was eating the soup she had just made him for lunch, and he now looked up with uncertainty, and little tears formed in his eyes when Jonathan said he was leaving.

"But all my friends are here," Jake cried.

Ellen chimed in. "He can stay, you know. His grandmother can visit. It will not be a problem."

"I am afraid it really is not that simple, Ellen," Jonathan said.

Those words were said with finality and so it was that Jake was piled into a buggy and on his way to a new life in another community. A part of her always knew this would happen but she had hoped maybe this was the plan Gott had for her life. Now here she was again, locking herself into her house and crying.

Minutes later, Ruth brought Able by to play with Jake. Ellen was too heartbroken to open the door or to tell them that he had been taken away from her. There would be plenty of time for that later. In fact, she was sure that they would hear long before she had a chance to tell them. For that reason, she remained quietly in the house and waited for them to leave.

"Maybe they went to the fields," Able said.

Ellen smiled. If only that were the case. She sighed, bathed and went to bed at two in the afternoon. When she crawled out of bed the next day, she knew exactly what she had to do.

Sadness

Jubilation was an understatement for what Mary was feeling. Rebecca, the lady who managed the schoolhouse, had just told her that she could now help in the schoolhouse full time. The cold, rainy summer breeze nipping around her would have caused her to rush right home on a regular day. Today was no such day.

"What are you so happy about?" Anna came skipping to her side to ask. She had almost forgotten that her friend was to be visiting her parents.

She giggled, unable to control herself before answering. Mary jumped with joy before turning her eyes towards the heavens and shouting a glorious thank-you.

"I get to be a teacher, Anna!" she shouted to her friend. "I get to start on Monday!"

They erupted in a hugging ball of delightful squeals and pats on the back. Overcome with excitement, they made their way up the hill from the barn house, parting ways only then to go home. Mary had always wanted to work in the schoolhouse. It might not have seemed like such a big deal to most, but it was for her. A teaching job might be no different to working in a restaurant catering to the tourists or working in the town to most people. For most people those jobs were just jobs, what was required to help them make it from day to day, but not for Mary.

Walking up the lane that took her to the humble cottage she shared with Amos, she couldn't help but remember the days when she would sit on her parents' porch and watch the teachers, wishing to be one of them. For as long as she could remember, she knew she wanted to work with the children and not just as a nursery help. No, she wanted to play a role in the *imparting of knowledge* as her mother so aptly put it. Teaching not only required the necessary skills, but also that those in charge recognized who had those said skills.

She was elated.

"Mamm! Daed!" she called out aloud as she ran past her house and on to her parents' home. In that moment, she was not the grown mature woman many prided her on being. Today she was just a regular child, excited to tell her parents her good news.

"Where is your coat?" her mamm asked her. "You will catch the cold walking out in the rain."

It was only then that Mary realized that she had come all the way without her coat. It didn't matter.

"I got the teaching post, Mamm!" she said with a big grin as her mamm threw a warm blanket over her shoulders and pulled her in for a hug.

"I knew you would, Dochder. I knew you would."

Her father was a man of very few words but the pride in his eyes as he beamed down at her said enough.

"I have to go tell Amos!"

She didn't even wait for them to consent, and she could hear her mother's proud laugh behind her. This time she didn't leave without the blanket, or she might very well have caught cold. Autumn was around the corner, and this winter was going to be horrid; she could tell. It was only early August and the town had seen way more rainfall than was usual, and the kind of wind that would freeze you solid if you stood still too long. With that in mind, she rushed over to her house, hoping Amos was done working early.

The thought brought a smile to her face. He had always told her she would get the job. There had never been any doubt for him.

"Amos!" she called as she walked to the back of the house where his small stable was. He had been busy putting up boards to fill the spaces he had created to keep the horses cool during summer.

"Back here!" he called.

She turned the corner and smiled at the dirt stain on his cheeks and a bead of sweat rolling down his forehead.

"I got the teaching post. I start on Monday."

He laughed at her Cheshire grin and pulled her to him. "I told you that you would."

As his strong arms wrapped around her, she closed her eyes and felt that all was right with the world. Soon they would be married and her mamm could stop hinting at her that she expected babies soon.

"There is something I need to talk to you about though, Mary," he whispered into her kapp.

She stepped back at the concern that echoed throughout the barn. "What is it?"

"Maybe not now." He smiled down at her and tucked a stray strand of hair behind her ear.

The sadness in his eyes was undeniable. "No, tell me what's wrong."

"Oh. Of course nothing is wrong." He smiled and kissed her cheek. "I was just thinking that maybe we should start preparing the house for our child. I know we will soon have one. I can just feel it."

With all the excitement of the day, Mary felt her head swim with joy. But before she could respond to him, her legs gave way and she crumbled as darkness consumed her. The last thing she could hear was Amos calling her name, the worry in his voice evident. She tried to tell him she was okay, but no words came out of her mouth. She felt his strong arms lift her up and, as the blackness completely took over, she felt his strong powerful strides and the breeze on her face as if he had lifted her and was carrying her to safety.

She smiled then as she drifted off. She really loved this man.

Bundle of Joy

"*No, no, no!*" *Mary muttered in her sleep. The familiar feeling of hopelessness overwhelmed her and blanked her senses. Her chest tightened and her mind went back to the helpless feeling she had as a child. Claustrophobia overwhelmed her and she couldn't think straight. All she could see was her imminent death, and her mind refused to help her find her way out.*

Trapped! Somewhere in the nightmare she knew it wus just a dream, but she couldn't wake herself. She was trapped.

That was the only thought she had, and it was one that came from a place she was not even sure of. Beads of sweat broke out on her forehead and it wasn't the heat that caused her to sweat. Images of the flames flashed in her mind and she could almost feel the heat of the flames that were coming up the ladder for her. The fear that crippled her was taking its toll and if she sat there any longer, death would have its way.

"Mary!" She heard her mamm's voice breaking

through the abyss of despair. "Where are you, Dochder?"

The urgency of the call made her scream out, and her mother's arms pulled her to safety.

"Stay right here," her mother ordered. The white dress her mother wore was burnt in places and covered in soot in others.

"No, Mamm," Mary begged her. "Don't go back in there."

Her mother smiled down at her. "It's okay, Mary. It will all be okay."

Her mother's voice trailed off in the strong winds that blew, and Mary watched helplessly as her mother went into the burning barn once again. Mary screamed for her to come back, but she didn't. And as she watched, the roof collapsed, and she screamed as loud as she could.

Mary bolted upright in bed, clutching at the strong arms that held her up and brushed her hair from her face.

"Mary, it's okay," Amos said as a cold rag was pressed to her feverish face.

She was disoriented for a few seconds but when she finally got her bearings, she realized she was staring at Anna's worried face and her parents were right there. In the corner, Ruth held a frightened Able, and Mary raised a questioning brow as to why he was in the room.

"We were coming to bring you a piece of the cake he baked for you when we saw Amos rushing to you and you crying out for your mamm."

She smiled down at her worried son. "Come here."

He looked hesitant but then climbed onto the bed with her.

"You okay?" Able asked, resting a palm against her cheeks.

Her eyes swam with tears as she looked down into his worried eyes. He was just perfect. She knew every mother thought that of their kinner, but she knew beyond a doubt that her son was; unconventional birth or not.

"I don't know if I am," she said, kissing the top of his head and deciding to be honest with him. "I hope so."

Just then the doctor walked in and before she could speak more, he ushered everybody but Amos and Mary out of the room. His examination took fifteen minutes and when he was done, he smiled at them.

"I believe you are with child, Mary," he said.

The couple looked at him as if he had just spoken in some language they did not understand.

"I'm sorry," Mary said, barely able to speak. "What did you say?"

He smiled at them both and spoke. "Don't look so terrified. If I am right, you now have what you have always wanted. You might need to confirm that with a specialist, though. An Englisch doctor visits the town next door on Wednesdays. I could send for him within the hour. I will clear it with the bishop."

With that, he stepped out and Amos, as always knowing what she needed without her saying so, opened the door to tell the others they shouldn't be worried and that she would be okay, but she needed some time. For the next hour, she remained silent, drifting in and out of sleep as Amos lay beside her watching her every breath. Two hours later they answered a knock at the door, to find a doctor dressed in Englisch clothes. He introduced himself as Aaron and went on to examine her. Five minutes later he confirmed their suspicions.

"Yes, Mary." He smiled. "You are with child. My advice to you is to take it easy. You need to not overexert yourself and you should eat healthy foods, though you Amish have no problem with that. It is a thing I envy."

They laughed and Amos jokingly said he could move into the community. After giving her a course of prenatal vitamins and stern warnings, he left the room for her parents to enter. Mary beamed at them. There was no way she could contain that joy anymore.

"I am pregnant, Mamm!" she blurted out and her mother rushed to her side and pulled her into her arms.

"I told you, Dochder, Gott's plans can never be rushed."

Mary cried tears of joy and rested a protective hand over her stomach. Amos's hand covered hers and she drifted back to sleep with a smile and renewed hope for the future.

Later that evening, she dressed, and they decided to join the house church for a small service. Ruth and Samuel joined them, and the haus was filled with members of the community, gathered together to listen to the word of Gott and to worship together.

After the service, while everyone was talking and catching up on news of the community, Ellen made her way over to Ruth. She asked if she might talk to her alone and the two women stepped outside onto the porch and sat down with a cup of kaffe.

"Ruth, when you found Able on your doorstep, what were your first thoughts?" Ellen asked.

"To get him inside and out of the cold," Ruth replied without hesitation.

"You must surely have known that whoever had placed him there was still close by?"

"Samuel did go out to look for any sign of anyone. If I recall, he even called out for whoever was there to make their presence known. Why do you ask?"

"Gott led me to ask. Maybe He is uncertain of His choice for parents for the child."

Ruth gasped. How could this woman say such things? Not only was she assuming to suggest that Gott could be wrong, she was saying outright that Ruth and Samuel were not the right people to parent their sonn. Ruth found herself at a loss for words. Fortunately she was rescued by Amos and Able who stepped outside at that precise moment and joined the two women on the porch. Ellen excused herself and left the three Beilers alone outside.

"Is everything gut, Ruth?" Amos asked, concern evident in his voice.

Ruth feigned good humor and smiled across at him while lifting her sonn onto her lap. "You know that I love you both with all my heart and I thank Gott every day and every night for bringing you both into my life?"

"Jah, Mamm, we know that," Able confirmed while Amos tried to hide his amusement at his sonn's confidence in the love his parents had for him.

The three sat together on the porch, and a fidgety Able was filled with questions about what it would be like to have a baby sister of his own.

"It could be a boy," Amos kept reminding him, and each time Able would frown at him.

"Nope. It's a girl!"

"How are you so sure?" Amos asked him as they left church that evening.

"I want a baby sister to take care of and Ruth said that Gott provides, so I know it's a girl."

Somehow, Mary also assumed that he worried that another boy might replace him in the hearts of his parents. She needed to reassure him that they would always want him, and he would never be replaced.

"You know you will always be just as loved and important if I have a boy, right?" she asked him.

"You mean you won't replace me?" Able asked after careful consideration.

"Never!" both she and Amos reassured him.

He turned and looked at Ruth and Samuel, and while Ruth smiled and echoed what she had said, Samuel's eyes twinkled mischievously.

"Well, there is this horse I have been wanting for a while," he said placing his fingers on his chin. "I think I can exchange a healthy little boy for him."

He picked Able up and pretended to examine him.

"Yes, yes," Samuel said. "This boy here is healthy. I will exchange him for a horse in the morning."

"No!" Able screamed with laughter as Samuel tickled him. "I am not healthy."

The little boy pretended to cough as a sign of his bad health but even that only garnered a bout of laughter.

"Able, tomorrow you will get your own horse. And tomorrow you will also learn how to care for the horse yourself," Samuel informed him.

Able was about as happy as a pup with two tails as he leapt off his mamm's lap and threw himself onto his daed. "My own horse!"

"I think you have proven that you are responsible enough to look after your own horse now. Since you will be a big bruder to Mary's boppli when it arrives, it is just as well that you learn how to care for others now."

Mary looked at them and felt so grateful. Her story could have turned out so much worse.

As was customary, on two of the four days she saw Able, she and Amos would put him to bed. They climbed the stairs and got him ready. As always, he wanted to read the book his Auntie Megan had given him; the one about the train that saved a little boy and his dog. At the end of the story he would always ask if he could have a dog. He didn't know yet, but he would be getting just that in a few months on his birthday.

Many had questioned why Mary hadn't reclaimed her son once she was a fully baptized member of the community. Even more had assumed that Amos didn't want him, but Amos loved Able with every beat of his heart. She had watched her husband with the little boy and saw how the love flowed from everything Amos did, from teaching him to hammer nails to reading him stories at night. Able had settled in with the Beilers. He was loved and accepted by his parents, and they didn't keep Mary out of his life. He was fine, and it would be selfish of her to attempt to disrupt the good thing they had going on. It would be unfair to Able, and so this arrangement worked. She paid no attention to those who had other things to say about it.

When they kissed him good night and made their way home, Anna, who was visiting for the last harvest, rushed up to her.

"I'm so happy!"

Mary laughed. She was too, and words alone were not enough to express that.

"Able wants a sister," she told Anna, as Amos walked ahead of them to give them some privacy and open the doors for her.

"Of course he does. Ever the protective brother is what he will be," Anna laughed. "He is already so taken by Mary-Ann and has several suggestions of names for Megan's son. There is no way this little bundle of joy you carry will escape him."

They laughed.

"Did you ever think that, after everything, we would be here today?" Mary asked Anna as her friend hugged her goodnight.

"I hoped it," Anna said. "I believed it too, but to live it brings a different kind of joy that I have never experienced before. It all worked out, Mary. It all worked out."

Mary smiled as she walked up the stairs to where Amos was waiting at the doorway. He kissed her forehead as she walked into the house, and they prepared for bed.

"Are you feeling okay?" Amos asked her.

She smiled. "I have never been better."

That night, they held hands as they knelt by the side of their bed and prayed. They prayed in gratitude and to ask Gott to guide them as they looked to bring another life into this world. They drifted off to bed with talks about expanding the two small rooms into one for their boppli. Amos was particularly excited, and Mary smiled at the joy in his voice. Her last thought was thanks to Gott, and she let the weariness rock her to sleep.

Bringing Gifts

A few houses over, a sinister thought was in the process of becoming a reality. With the pain of all that was happening in her life, Ellen was about to break. She threw a shawl over her shoulders to ward off the cool late summer night breeze, and she stepped out of her house and into the darkness. She looked up and down the lane before she made a move. Ellen was not expecting anyone to be around at that hour. She had purposely waited until it was extremely late. This was usually the hour those children slipping away for rumspringa fun would be making their way to the roads, but the night around her was silent.

Quietly stepping down the wooden stairs, she turned left behind her house and into the woods. Not wanting to get lost in the dark, the woman slung the backpack she had been carrying across her back and followed the creek. By her count, she had five hours before sunrise. That meant she had to leave where she was heading in four hours. She walked purposefully and as quietly as she could towards the little cottage that was an hour's walk into the woods. Her husband had taken her there once when they had been out wandering the forest, and the rain had caught them. That had been over ten years ago, but she knew it wouldn't be run down. It had been built of concrete and built well too. They had often wondered who had built it because it simply stood in the woods unbothered by everything around it. It wasn't to be used for long, though. For what she was planning, she just needed a place for a few days.

She reached the little cottage and stood in confusion for a moment. Her eyes adjusted to the darkness and the sliver of moonlight that was her salvation showed her that the undergrowth had all but covered the house she was searching for.

"Oh wow!" she whispered in delight. It was the perfect camouflage and she knew that no one would think to look for her this far into the woods. She walked around to the door of the cottage and was grateful that the summer rains had not done too much damage. She decided not to use the knife she carried to cut away the bush, but simply pushed it aside to open the door. It took a bit of effort, and the musky scent that greeted her was evidence that the place had been locked up for a while.

She walked into the space that was a lot bigger than it appeared from the outside and smiled. The small cupboards were covered in cobwebs and the floor was devoid of anything but dust. It was perfect. She went back out into the dark and picked branches to be used as a broom. She smiled as she spent the next two hours cleaning, using the rags she had brought with her. She walked a short distance to the creek to gather water, and then cleaned some more. When she had the place clean, she cracked the old windows and aired the inside. She sat and thought about her next move, before walking back home before the first signs of sunrise.

The following morning, she made her way to the schoolhouse where Mary was starting her first day. Ellen avoided the bubbly, pregnant young woman as much as she could but that was impossible in such a small space.

"It's nice to see you out and about today, Ellen," Mary said, approaching her.

Ellen smiled and nodded before stepping away to tend to her group of children. This was once a task she loved, but not so much anymore. No so much at all. The children also seemed to avoid her, and little Able, who had always been a bit wary of her, kept his distance. It made her wonder if something had been said to him. She doubted that. Ignoring it, she went about her business and when the schoolhouse was out for the day, she quickly slipped away, taking the long route that would allow her to get home without seeing Ruth, who was likely on her way to pick up Able.

Later that night, she returned to the cottage. This time though, she rolled up the soft rubber mat her husband used to love to lie on top of on the ground and packed it with a few more things. As she neared the cottage, she heard chatter.

She almost gave herself away out of anger, but when she saw two young Amish lovers happily examine the hideout she had been hoping to claim for herself, she contained her anger long enough to walk back home. Her plans had to change.

* * *

The following day she made a choice to visit the farm house her parents had left her when they died. It was a thirty-minute walk, but she hitched her buggy and went that way just as the sun was coming up. She passed Old Mr. Raber's apple orchards that were speckled with color and ready for harvesting. He was her closest neighbor. It was one of the reasons why after she had gotten married, they had decided to move into her husband's house. Being surrounded by family and friends was what they had both wanted, but now she felt she could use the space.

She got to the house and unpacked the buggy. Just after dusk, she took a walk over to Mr. Raber to see how he was doing. She figured that it would be best to ensure that he saw her there days before she put her plan into motion. She didn't want the unnecessary attention later. She chopped two sticks of cane from the backyard and walked the ten minutes over to his place. He was a stocky old man who smiled for no one but his grandchildren, both of whom had decided the Englisch world was where they wanted to spend the rest of their lives. They visited often, and before she had moved in with her husband, she remembered having a great many apple pies from his kitchen. His wife had died some years ago, but with a steady influx of farm hands, the place looked unaffected and his produce was even more so.

"Mr. Raber!" she called.

"Who's that?" the gritty deep voice called back from somewhere in the house.

"It is Ellen Hertzler. I come bringing gifts."

There was a long pause as if he was considering whether to chase her off his property or say hello. In the end the door opened, and after expressions of seemingly genuine surprise, she was invited in for tea. She left a few hours later with a basket of apples and a freshly baked apple pie. The guest she would soon have would appreciate them both beyond words.

Thanks

It was late the following day before Mary ventured out of her house to carry out her usual tasks. She was avoiding, actively avoiding, to preserve her sanity. The nausea was much worse today, and she didn't know if it was because of her pregnancy or the food she had eaten the day before. When she made her way to the school-house, it was with slow careful steps, afraid she might empty her stomach on the roadside. Maybe she should have stayed home after such a long night, but she had just been given this job and she was not about to slack off. Somehow her disposition improved during the day. She was certainly distracted by the kinners in her class and the manner in which they responded to her teaching. She was going to miss the kinners when she stayed home to look after the boppli.

Despite having improved as the day wore on, she was more than ready to head home at the end of the school day. The pregnancy was tiring her out beyond explanation, and she just wanted to get home and put her feet up before having to make the evening meal.

"Hey, Mary!" a bubbly Chrisanne called to her as she was walking home from work.

"Hey, Chrisanne!" she called with a smile, happy for the distraction from the madness inside her. "How are you?"

The bubbly girl with the freckled face and a waistline a size more than the average was all too happy to entertain her. "I am fine. You know my sister just had her first baby, so it has been nothing but a lot of fun at the house. You should come around some time."

She smiled but didn't answer. Chrisanne had only good intentions. She was Mary's oldest friend, besides Anna.

"And your mamm?" she asked of the ailing woman who had been the joy of the community for as long as she could remember. Chrisanne's mother had always managed to make those wonderful treats they all looked forward to, and Chrisanne seemed to have consumed one too many. Not that it mattered to Mary. She liked Chrisanne for nothing more than the consistent friend she had been.

"My mamm is doing okay," Chrisanne said with a worried look that flashed across her face. "She has that terrible cough that does not seem to be leaving, but she is up and about, cooking as per usual."

They laughed for nothing was closer to the truth than that statement. But as the laughter passed, an awkward silence took its place.

"Are you okay, Mary? You seem different," Chrisanne asked with piercing eyes. Mary knew she would have a hard time hiding from the eyes that searched for the answers to questions not yet asked. She looked at her friend wishing she could really tell her what was on her mind but knowing she could never burden her with such a tale. She instead nodded.

"I have been feeling a little under the weather, but I am okay."

That was an understatement, and as she said it, her eye itched.

"Tell me if it is something that maybe I can help you with," Chrisanne said. "You know I am here for you, don't you? Always."

It was a sweet gesture and one that eased the coming headache just a little. "I know, Chrisanne, and I am ever grateful. Why don't you walk home with me and you can tell me all about what's happening in your life over a lemonade on our porch?"

Chrisanne welcomed the opportunity to talk about herself and the young mann she was courting now. In the hour that they spent rocking back and forth together on the porch, Amos served them lemonade and cookies and her father came by to see how they were doing. Chrisanne enchanted her with tales of budding love. When dusk fell and Chrisanne excused herself to go home she was relieved, but it did not last for long.

The footsteps that echoed along the stone path leading up to their house were enough to tell her they had yet another visitor. When the black hat appeared in the glow of the lantern hanging from the porch, she felt a strange tingle run down her spine before she even knew the reason.

"Good evening, Mary," Brett said timidly from the bottom of the stairs. Her heart skipped a few beats and she forgot how to speak. "Cassandra sent me by with some goodies to say thanks for the help you offered for the feast."

Brett lived down the lane in the little cottage belonging to Sister Cassandra, the friendly old woman who had taken to him when he had moved there. He had left his Amish community after his parents had died, he found it peaceful here. Cassandra's house was called the Quiet Cottage, and Mary had often thought how she had never heard a sound coming from the haus in all the years.

"Hello," she said. She could see his eyes twinkle at seeing her and her face flushed in response. She thought that was strange but brushed it off as she noticed for the first time just how attractive he was. He wasn't just one of those men you could call handsome. His piercing eyes and sleek jawbone somehow softened his features in a masculine way, making him even more attractive and manly. But no man around could compare to her Amos. Not even this one who had said time and time again that he liked her. She had never been interested at all.

Amos opened the door and joined them on the porch and it was not long before Brett excused himself. Although the lemonade had settled her stomach as had Chrisanne's conversation, she knew Amos would realize immediately that she wasn't feeling well.

"Do you want to lie down, or would you like to take a walk to the creek with me?"

He asked not out of inconsideration, but more so out of knowing that dipping her feet in the cool water often held some panacea for her.

She happily accepted the offer, anticipating the

calming effect of the water on her body and soul. She went inside to collect her shawl and Amos stood with his hands in his pockets, waiting for her at the bottom of the stairs. They did not say a word to each other. Each caught up in thinking about what should be said. She walked a few steps with him to the river that ran through the community and stopped beneath the almond tree. She took a deep breath and turned her head to the skies, looking at the slivers of moonlight that peeped through the leaves, and took a deep breath. It instantly settled her soul. There in the darkness that swallowed her secrets, she turned to the man she had invited into her life.

An owl screeched overhead, and the night crickets sang their chorus, but all she could hear was her heart beating its way to its death, and as Amos stood before her, she lost what little control she had over herself.

He stepped up to her without a word and pulled her towards him, and with the whispering of secrets that should not be told, he gently pressed his lips to hers and removed any doubt of what he felt for her. The electricity passing between them could have earned them a one-way ticket to an inferno, but in that moment she did not care. There they stood on the bank of the rushing river, cloaked in darkness, sharing a moment that epitomized their life together.

Somewhere, a twig broke but it did not bother them.

"I love you, Mary. Thanks for making me the happiest man alive."

She leaned into him and all the sickness she had felt earlier vanished as his arms held her close and the river rushed by.

A Beautiful Day

Mary woke to the sound of excitement all around her. Georgia from next door had asked her to look out for her little son Michael while she helped in the barn house, preparing for tonight's harvest festival. When they had come to collect him, he was fast asleep, so they let him stay for the night.

He didn't want to go to the early harvest service and so she let him hide out in the house. He signaled from the barn that his parents were on their way back from church and as soon as she saw that, she sent him on his way and headed down to Ruth's house where she had work to do. Today had been declared a feast day by the bishop and so there was no need to cook. Ruth was however having Anna and her parents over for dinner and so they had invited her too. Amos would come later. Brett was already there.

Mary was happy, because all was right with world. Something she never once thought she would have been able to say.

"Can I come?" Michael hollered after her.

"Ask your mamm when you get there!" she called back to him and walked off with him saying he would.

Just then Amos walked up behind her. "Hello, my love," he said, kissing her on the back of her head, before rubbing her growing stomach.

She felt that strange tingling again that only happened when Amos walked by. It was as if her whole body came alive when he was around. It told her she was attracted to him. She chuckled and walked away as Amos smiled at her playfully. She kept thinking that with time that would change, but it had not as yet, not at all.

"Thanks for coming," Ruth said, rushing to the door and breaking up their very awkward moment. "Let me put you right to work peeling this mountain of potatoes."

She was ushered away with a fleeting smile from Brett that told her something she wasn't quite sure of. Casting one last glance back at him, she followed Ruth, who was now speaking to no one in particular about all the work they had to do before the feast could begin in just five hours. Behind her, Amos hung in the background, but his presence was welcomed. For the next hour as she worked, Mary would look at him; stealing glances when she assumed he had no idea she was looking at him.

He really was handsome. The kind of innocent beauty she wasn't so sure existed anymore. She loved him more with each passing day.

"You do know you are married to him, right?" She heard a familiar yet barely audible whisper in her ear. She jumped, blushing to see Michael's smiling face beside her. She had been so lost in thought she had not even heard him walk in.

"Shhh!" she shushed him and he smiled. "What are you doing here?"

"Mamm said I could come help," he said with a frown. "I asked like you told me to, and she said it is okay."

The hint of disappointment in his face at the tone of her voice made her regret how harshly she had just spoken to him, and so she tousled his hair in apology and smiled as he took a seat beside her and began peeling potatoes. How much she had been enjoying his company, she would never be able to explain.

"He is quite the catch," he whispered with a smile, and Mary went back to admiring Amos who was now laboring over the dough he was kneading. It was strange around these parts to see a man handling a woman's work so well, but here he was doing just that and in so doing adding to his appeal. But she had to look at her little brother sideways, wondering what he knew about this dating world. But then again, she spoke to him about such things.

She turned her attention back to Amos, noticing everything about him. The way he furrowed his brows in concentration and wrinkled his nose as the flour teased a sneeze out of him. She noticed the way he shifted from one foot to the next as if he was nervous and tapped a foot in time to the rhythm of the task he was doing. She noticed the way his eyelashes flittered coyly as if flirting with the dough that would soon be consumed as pastry. She noticed it all.

And then Amos lifted his eyes for a moment from

the task at hand and glanced her way. Their eyes met in silent conversation and her breath left her in a startled whisper as she recognized something in his eyes. It was not curiosity at the fact that he had just caught her looking at him. It was not aversion, nor was it surprise. It was joy and with it came the silent words that said *I see you too.*

"He likes you too," said Michael from beside her as he caught the exchange between them. Ever the astute one, Mary knew he would not have missed it. "That's good."

"He had better." She pinched Michael's cheeks. "I married him, remember?" she told him without taking her eyes from the man who captivated her. He laughed and kept peeling potatoes.

"My mother and father look at each other the same way. Someday I will have a woman I look at like that too. Until then I will just peel these potatoes."

Mary laughed. "You had better!"

It was not a command to get him to be silent, but rather one to ensure that his utterance did not take from her the moment they were sharing.

A few seconds later, Amos smiled and lowered his eyes back to the flour board before him, and Mary nearly peeled the skin from her own hand in joy. She didn't know how, but then and there she was well aware that she was so connected with someone on a level that was simply surreal. She didn't care about anything else. Only him and the child growing inside her.

She playfully groaned out loud. "Here we go again."

Michael looked at her worriedly. "What is the matter?"

"I like him," she said.

"I know."

She smiled again. "He likes me?"

Michael nodded, glancing at Amos, who was again looking at Mary with a smile. "Yes, he does."

"I think he noticed." She nodded a chin towards her husband standing to the side of the kitchen with a sweet smile on his face. No one had noticed him walk in through the side door.

"Oh," Michael said, his eyes widening with mischief. "I think that might be a problem."

Mary laughed again and kissed the little boy's forehead. "Someday you will make a woman the happiest woman alive."

"And make bopplin?" he asked.

"Yes," she nodded. "And make beautiful bopplin."

They passed the next hour talking about whatever topic Michael raised, and when they were finished with the potatoes, Able burst through the door and her Amos scooped him up, turned him upside down and dipped him in the flour he was supposed to be working. Able squealed with delight before Ruth and Mika slapped Amos on the arms for wasting their flour. When Amos set him down, Able ran over to her and gave her a kiss on the cheek before standing beside Michael and shaking all the flour out of his hair on him. Michael forgot what he was doing and the two dashed outside to play.

Amos sat beside her to finish what Michael had started. When the pies for the festival were safely in the oven, Ruth and Samuel served their guests a light dinner. The boys were brought back inside for the meal with the promise that they could play outside after they had cleaned their plates.

"We won't overfeed you so that you can't enjoy the food at the festivities tonight," Ruth said, "but we wanted to celebrate the harvest and Mary and Amos's bundle of joy that will soon be with us."

Anna's baby girl, who had been sleeping upstairs, cried out and Evan got up to fetch her. He came back down, and Ruth continued to speak with happiness while tears of joy spilled down her face. Able reached over to wipe them. It was a beautiful day.

Little did they know, that would soon change.

Happiest Man Alive

Mary nearly jumped out of her skin in the dark while she collected the linen from the wash line. She had reminded her mother that they were out there, but the older woman must have forgotten. She had washed them earlier in the day and asked her mother to take them inside on her way back from the barn house.

"I know now." She heard Amos's voice behind her and managed to stifle a scream just in time.

"Dear Lord! You nearly caused me to meet my death! What are you doing out here? I thought you were helping down by the creek with the setting up."

He slowly walked over to her. "So, what I thought to be true really is?"

"What?" she asked him in surprise.

He smiled at her, but she didn't know what to make of it. "Your truth, Mary. I know all about it. Your truth is hidden but it is there, and I have thought it for a long time."

"Yes, you have discovered my truth," she said, laughing at him.

"I saw the way you looked at me today," he said.

She looked at him with his hands in the pocket of his breeches, waiting on her to say something. It was a defiant stance that oozed the tenderness he could not hide.

"I am so in love with you, Amos," she exaggerated.

"Oh, I know. Michael told me."

"That little tattletale!"

He laughed. "Just you be careful it doesn't become your undoing," he said and walked away.

He picked up the basket of linen she had just collected and walked into the house ahead of her. There they got ready for the night ahead.

Had they bothered to look into the darkness, they would have noticed they were not alone.

A Sinister Thought

When Ellen got to the house, she took out the things she had placed in the buggy. She opened the doors and pushed the thought of her parents aside as she went about cleaning the house. By the time dusk fell, the house was in pristine condition and the Bermuda grass that had been overgrown would be tackled when she woke up the following day. For now, she decided that she didn't need to go back to the community. She would spend the night where she was and see how she felt the next day. The harvest festival would be in two days, she needed everything ready for then.

The entire community was embroiled in preparing for the harvest festival over those two days. Since the routines were not in place and life was not as normal for anyone who was Amish thereabouts, it was not surprising that Ellen Hertzler's sinister thoughts would so easily manifest as reality. She had watched Michael take the smaller boy outside to play after they had eaten their meals the night before. This would be like taking candy from a baby.

"Michael," she had admonished him in a commanding voice. "Your mother says you are to get home this minute. It is very late, and she was expecting you home before now."

Michael looked sheepishly at Able, embarrassed at having been scolded in front of the little boy who looked up to him as a superior. "Denke, I will go tell Mary I am leaving."

"Nee, don't waste more time and cause your poor mamm any more distress. Go now. I will tell Mary, and I will tell Ruth you said denke for the meal. Go now," Ellen urged the hesitant child.

Michael did not want to assume to question an adult. He also was in two minds about leaving without saying good bye to the family he was visiting with. Ellen's look made up his mind for him. He realized that he was mistaken in thinking that he had a part to play in the decision. "Good night, Able. I will see you in the morning."

"Gut night, Michael. Denke for the gut time today," Able responded.

Ellen had to move quickly now before Able slipped into the haus and she lost the opportunity. She only had this one chance and she dare not mess it up. She removed the damp cloth from her apron pocket, put her arm casually about Able's shoulder, and slipped the cloth over his mouth. It was a gut thing that she still had the morphine the doctor had given for her husband to take during the last days of his illness. The child soon relaxed against her, all resistance futile in the face of the strong drug. She lifted the supine form and carried him to the buggy she had parked behind the barn. With the child asleep on her lap she rode quietly to the farm haus in which she had been raised as a kind. Could she possibly now be free to raise the gift that had been denied her when the Beilers wrongfully took possession of the boppli that Gott intended to be hers and her husband's.

She stopped the buggy as close to the door of the long-vacated farm haus as possible and carried the sleeping child into the haus. She had spent the past day decorating his room as she would have any sonn she may have birthed herself had Gott seen so fit. She tucked the little form into the bed and covered him with the quilt she had made as a newly married fraa so many years ago, intended for her first boppli. Now all was right with the world. The errors had been corrected and Gott would smile down on her. A movement to the side of the room caught her eye and she looked up in fright to focus on it. Her dear husband was looking down at the sleeping sonn he had never had the opportunity to father, and he looked so happy.

"I am sorry, Liebling, that I could not do this for you before now," she directed to the form before the window. In response the form simply nodded a head and smiled at her. She knew then that she had done what was right and expected of her.

The exhaustion was overwhelming, and Ellen suddenly felt unable to take another step. She would sleep right here on the floor beside her sonn, in the room where her Liebling was also. Together they would watch over their sonn as he slept the sleep of peacefulness.

* * *

That peacefulness would only last as long as he was asleep. As soon as his eyes opened the following morning, he stared in confusion at Ellen's face smiling down at him.

"Where is my mamm?" he asked, rubbing the sleep from his eyes.

Ellen had not thought much about what her response would be if he had indeed asked that, but she was thinking about it now. She was sure she wouldn't come up with an answer he would accept, but she decided that whatever answer she gave would simply have to be acceptable.

"Well, Able," she began, walking closer to the little boy. "Your mamm and daed are at home."

"Okay," he said, unbothered. "Can you take me to them now? I am supposed to work the stables with Daed today. We got a new horse he says will be mine. Today I will learn to take care of him."

She sighed and looked down at his expectant face. "I can't do that, Able,' she replied softly.

His five-year-old brows furrowed in confusion, and she knew that if she didn't give him a reasonable excuse, his confusion would turn to anger.

"They do not want you anymore," she said flatly. "That was what your mother and I were speaking about last night when you and your father came in. They just can't care for you anymore and so they told me to come and collect you."

"Not true!" he shouted, and the tears welled up in his eyes. She tried to hug him, but the little boy was just not having it. "I want to go home now!"

Ellen stared at him helplessly. She expected the tears, but she had never counted on how adamant and angry he would be.

"Let's have some breakfast and then we will see about that," she said to him. "You can maybe take some with you, if you can go."

She watched him decide and he seemed to decide that it was better to comply with her request on the off chance that he would then be allowed to leave, rather than to keep screaming in anger. He was a smart little boy. Ellen knew that.

"Why would my parents give me to you instead of back to Mary if they didn't want me?" he asked around the mouthful of sandwich he was eating.

"Well, Mary is about to have another child. You know there will be no space for you there."

Able put his food down. "That's not true either, Amos told me I can come by and stay with my baby sister whenever I want after she is born. They wouldn't give me away."

"They changed their minds. Adults do that a lot and I have this big house where you can play all day," she said.

"Will my friends be able to come here?"

She mistook that as his resignation to the fact. "Sure! You can make new friends. The old ones live a little far away from here."

"You mean I am not in the community?" he asked, frantically getting up and peering through the window. All he would see was green fields and, in the distance, Mr. Raber's apple orchards.

"Auntie Ellen," he said softly as tears slipped down his face. "I want to go home."

He allowed her to hug him this once, but it did not garner the response she wanted. "You can't, Able. Your parents gave you to me. It is hard now, but you will love it here and maybe in a couple of months we can move elsewhere for you to go back to a schoolhouse and make some friends."

He walked back to the table and cried. He cried almost all morning, and then fell asleep out of exhaustion by eleven. When he woke in the afternoon, she could still see the melancholy in his eyes, but he didn't ask about going home again. Instead he asked her to read a book and then stated what he wanted for dinner. When they were finished cooking, he helped to clean the kitchen and then said he was tired.

Ellen wanted to read him a book before bed, like she had dreamt of doing when she finally had children, but she didn't push him. She left him alone and watched as he cleaned up for bed. She sat at the top of the stairs until he had fallen asleep and then she took a bath and did the same. She smiled and thought this was the beginning of a new life for them both.

He would get better as the days passed. For now, she would let him decide how he wanted to handle everything. Including whatever they would do. Tomorrow, she was sure it wouldn't be safe to take him out the house, but she would do many fun things with him inside. She was hoping that by the end of the week, he wouldn't miss his parents too much. He had already stopped asking about them, so maybe there was hope for that indeed.

Find Him

Mary had not slept even a wink the night before. That was impossible when her son had been missing a full twenty-four hours. There were no clues in the house or even outside to point her in the direction he might have gone. There was literally nothing there. It was as if he had vanished.

Amos walked back into the house, his feet covered in mud and his face looking as haggard as was expected.

"Nothing?" she asked him, trying to contain her tears.

He shook his head. "And we looked everywhere, Mary."

"Did you check the creek?" she asked softly, dreading the little boy might have been sleepwalking, or thought it cool to go out on an adventure at night and had met his demise. He had not yet learned how to swim. They had planned on teaching him the next summer.

He nodded. "He wasn't there. We followed it all the way through the woods. There weren't even footprints."

Mary sighed. She wasn't so sure if it was out of relief or frustration, but the one thing she was sure of was that it was time to enlist more help.

"We need to call the state police in on this, Amos. It is good that the entire community and our neighbors have all pitched in, but maybe we need more people and we need more expertise." Her voice broke. "The longer he is out there, who knows what will happen to him."

He rushed to her and pulled her in for a hug. Just yesterday they were making plans for his sixth birthday, and now she was worried that she might need to be planning a funeral. The thought broke her. She wondered how much more he would have to endure as he grew up, praying that he got the chance to. She did not want to be one of those mothers who ended up putting their kinner's face on a milk carton for the next twenty years. She couldn't be one of those mothers, and she refused to believe her son would become another one of those statistics.

Amos left her to go to the bishop's house to make a phone call to the police. It was the only place with a phone for emergency purposes, and this was as big an emergency as they had ever had. She watched him hop on his horse and gallop down the road in urgency. Looking on, one would never have been able to tell that Able was not his biological child. Today he was the most important person in the entire community and the show of numbers for the search proved that. In every direction, she could hear people calling his name. Mary had been on the first search, but the fact that she was pregnant did not make it easy for her. She had to take it easy. She was warned not to put her unborn child at risk.

Her head snapped up as she saw Ruth and Samuel Beiler walking hand in hand towards her. She smiled at them as they approached but realized that her smile was not returned.

"Is everything okay?" she asked, fearing the worst.

"Can we talk inside?" Ruth asked.

It was not sadness she heard in the woman's voice. It was anger.

"Okay, Mary," Ruth came out saying. "Enough of the games. Where is he?"

Mary looked at her in confusion. "A-Amos, you mean? He went to the bishop to call the state police for more help."

"You know Amos is not who I am talking about," Ruth said, pacing the living room floor in anger. "You brought Able to us five years ago because you didn't want him."

"Now you stop right there!" Mary interrupted. "If you ever say I didn't want my child again, you will regret it."

She could handle any other misconceptions people might have, but this was not one she would tolerate and most certainly not from Ruth who knew far better. She would not have it at all.

"Where is he?!" Ruth demanded unapologetically. "We adopted him and still allowed you to stay in his life and you gave him up. And this is how you repay us. Where is my son?"

The realization of what Ruth was really implying suddenly hit her like a ton of bricks. She looked at the other woman in shock, but no words came out of her mouth. Mary now understood firsthand what it meant to be shocked beyond words.

"Tell me where my son is!" Ruth badgered her.

"Ruth…" Samuel urged, trying to get her to calm down.

Mary broke again. She reached for the closest chair she could find before her legs failed her.

"You think I would do this to my own child. A child I carried for nine hard months. A child I cried for every night after I gave him away. A child I loved more than myself; that I would suffer the loss just to give him the chance of a better life. You think that I would really do this to my own child?"

Ruth glared at her. "Because you want him back, yes!"

"Ruth!" Samuel said sternly this time and the woman backed away from her.

"Then you do not know me at all" was all Mary could say, as the tears streamed down her face.

Amos burst through the door. "Mary, they are comin…"

He stopped speaking when he saw the tears rolling down her face and an angry Ruth hovering like danger close by. "What's going on here?" Amos asked as he made his way to her side. No one answered him. The thought of repeating such a horrible accusation made Mary cringe.

"Somebody better tell me what's going on here right this minute," Amos demanded, looking at all three of them. Anna and Evan came through the door just then.

"It was a misunderstanding," Samuel said as he tried to steer his wife towards the door.

"Ruth thinks I kidnapped Able because I want him back," Mary said through her tears. She looked at the woman she had trusted with her son's life, but even though she was happy that Ruth was here fighting for him, her heart broke at the thought that she was actually thinking Mary was capable of endangering her own son.

"That is the most absurd thing I have ever heard!" Anna chimed in. "How could you, Ruth?"

"We already checked everywhere here, and Mary does not have a set of keys for your house, so how could she have possibly done that?" Amos said. "Why would she need to when you both live right there and we see him so often each week? Why would she do that and then come home? Where would she leave him? How would we raise a kidnapped child here?"

With each question Amos asked, his voice went up a few decibels. His face was becoming flushed and Mary saw anger flash in his eyes.

"Ruth," she said, not wanting things to blow out of proportion. "Understand that I love my child more than anybody else could possibly understand. I would never hurt him. I would never ever do something like this. That would make me selfish. So I ask that you redirect your efforts to helping us find him, so we can all sleep tonight. I didn't take him, and you are here trying to fight with me, while we have no idea where he is and what he might have to do to survive."

"True," Samuel chimed in softly. "We need to save the fighting for later. Right now, the most important thing is finding the little boy we all love so much."

Ruth still had a great deal of anger in her eyes, but for the moment she seemed convinced that Able was not here. She took a few steps away and walked through the door without another word. Mary's tears silently slipped down her cheek.

"I can't believe she could even fathom that I would do such a thing."

Evan was the one who pulled her in for a hug. "When our children are in danger, we are capable of heights of insane acts. I think Ruth knows you wouldn't, but you made her a mother and those instincts run deep."

Mary sniffled and Anna rubbed her back. "Let us just focus on finding him. I don't want him away from home for another night." She quickly made everyone an easy breakfast so they wouldn't be going back on the search with empty stomachs. When they were ready to leave, she put on her walking shoes and joined them.

"I think you should stay home," Amos urged gently.

She glared at him. "If you try to stop me from going through that door, you will be knocked right out."

He lifted his hands in surrender and watched as she walked by.

Able

All through the day, Able pretended to like the games his Auntie Ellen played, but he really was not interested. He was just biding his time. He did not believe a single word about his parents giving him away. He just did not believe it. He and his daed had plans for him to learn to ride a horse; before putting him to bed, his daed had promised he was big enough to work in the stables as long as he didn't get too close to the horses without supervision. He had been excited about it all, and then he woke up to the fact that they didn't want him.

He just did not believe it...

He was also worried that Ellen seemed very concerned with keeping the doors locked and the keys out of his reach. When he had asked her if they could go outside, she had told him no, that it was not safe. Peering through the window, he did not see a single thing out there that would hurt him.

He had to get home so his parents could explain everything to him. That night, he asked to go to bed early, knowing that she wouldn't go to her bed if he was still awake. After four hours, when he heard her softly snoring in her room, he pulled on his running shoes and softly crept past her bedroom door. Peering in, he realized she would not hear him over her own breathing unless he made a lot of noise. He went downstairs and to the back door, where a small box hole was cut into the door for a dog to come and go when the door was closed. He knew that because his friend Jonny had a big German Shepherd with just such a hole for him to walk through. This one looked smaller, but he knew he could fit. His mother was always telling him that he was small for his age, but that he would shoot right up when puberty hit.

He bent quietly and forced his head through the flap, and then the rest of his body slipped right through. He nearly screamed in delight when he was outside but remembered that he needed to make his getaway and he did not know where he was. He walked to the front of the house and saw a light in the distance, and as he dashed off towards it, he tumbled over a bucket that he had not seen. The commotion it made had surely woken Ellen, and a light came on in her bedroom. She poked her head out the window and, seeing him there, she hollered his name.

"Able! You get back in this house this instant!"

He didn't need any more encouragement. He dashed off towards the light in the distance. He ran as fast as his little feet could carry him. Falling a couple of times, he got right back up and kept running. He knew if Ellen ever caught up to him on her horse, it would be over for him. And it wasn't long before he heard the steady pounding of hooves. He dashed to the left into the apple orchards. He thought about climbing a tree, but that looked impossible for his tiny hands. Then he remembered how good Mary always said he was at hide and seek. He decided to play the best game of his life, so he stopped running just as Ellen got to the orchard on her horse. He didn't even know the poor old thing could run that fast. Able hoped that Ellen did not run him into the ground.

Hiding behind the trunk of a tree, he stayed still as she aimed her flashlight around frantically.

"Able, I know you are here," she called to him. "Come out and let's go back home. I promise I won't be angry."

He said nothing, but as the light turned away from where he was, he dashed four more trees over before stopping. He heard faint calls in the distance, but he couldn't tell if they were coming to get him too. He had never been in such a position before and he was trying his best to be as smart as his parents always said he was.

He waited again until the light turned and then he made a dash all the way to the end of the orchard. And the voices became clearer.

"Able!" he heard a man calling out. "Are you out here? Able! Your mother and father want you to come home. Able!"

He knew! He wanted to scream that but knew it would give his position away. In desperation, he made a run towards the voices and Ellen saw him.

"There you are!" she shouted as she turned her horse and chased after him, but Able was small and quick. He made it across the clearing dodging all Ellen's attempts to block him. When the torches and people searching for him were close enough, he screamed.

"Help! I'm over here! Help!"

"Able!" Mary's frantic voice sounded out from among the rest. "Able!"

"I'm over here!" he screamed and ran towards them. The tears were flowing down his face. He ran for his life and Ellen's horse was behind him. But she had no luck as he dashed right into Amos's arms and the man scooped him up and held him tight.

"Don't let her get me, Amos," he cried. "Don't let her get me!"

Amos held on to his small shivering frame and Mary kissed his cheeks, as if she couldn't believe he was there.

"Who, Able? Who shouldn't we let get you?"

More torches arrived and Able recognized the blue uniforms of police officers. His mamm had told him that, should he ever get in trouble and need help, these blue uniforms were the people who could help him.

"Aunt Ellen," he whispered through his tears. "She said none of you wanted me and Mamm and Daed gave me away. She said you didn't want me."

He broke down and cried and Mary took him from Amos. Able looked into his mother's eyes and saw nothing but love in the glimmer of the torch lights all around.

"You are loved, and you are wanted. I would have burnt this world to the ground to find you. Do not ever believe otherwise. You hear me?"

He nodded and turned his head into her chest. The sound of her heartbeat settled him, and the impatient whining of a horse drew their attention to the woman in the saddle a few feet away. Able watched as Ellen was about to turn and run, but the police officers grabbed her horse.

"This is your Auntie Ellen, Able?" they asked.

"Yes! And she is a mean old liar. She lied!"

"Shhhhh," Mary said as Ruth and Samuel burst through the clearing and scooped him up in their arms. They held him like there was no tomorrow and Ruth could not help the tears.

"You took my son, Ellen?" Mary's voice took on a cool and dangerous calm. "You really kidnapped a child who looked up to you as his loving aunt. You really did that?"

Silence settled around them and the police asked Ellen questions, but she would not answer.

"Able, can you tell us where you ran away from?" the man asked him.

"Yes, it is that house just beyond the orchards. It's big with lots of green space and the buggy is still un-hitched by the front."

"Take him home," the police officer ordered. "We will see to the rest."

Sweet Dreams

Two hours later, the community was in a state of joy and shock. Never in a million years did anybody, including Mary, think that Ellen was capable of such an act. They all spent that night at Ruth's house. And after two hours of apologizing, Mary and Ruth were friends again.

It was the perfect ending after two days of hell, and when the police came back, they found Ellen to have all that she would need to care for a five-year-old boy. They found the bed Able had slept in, and a screaming Ellen, who seemed to have suffered a mental breakdown, was taken into custody.

Although his face and hands had minor scratches from falling down, Able was just fine. The family had prayed thanks for his safe return before settling in that night. Mary looked at her sleeping son and knew that, had anything happened to him, she was not sure she would have survived.

When the lights were out, everyone in the Beiler house curled around Able on the mattresses in the living room. He was the first to fall asleep, his finger intertwined with Mary's little finger, and his other hand in Ruth's hair. He knew he was safe and sound, and the steady rise and fall of his chest was enough for comfort.

"Thank Gott," she whispered, kissing his small palm as she drifted off to sleep.

Two weeks later, the community held a barbecue to say goodbye to the hot summer days and prepare for autumn. It was a jubilant affair with much laughter and dancing. When Mary's legs tired of all the dancing, she whispered that she was taking a break in the room to the back of the bishop's house. Amos grabbed them each a plate of food and led her up the lane and to their house and into their room instead. It was soon after two in the morning and she was exhausted and hungry. He watched her eat while they spoke about all they would be doing come winter. When she was done, he gave her a kiss and rubbed his nose against hers, and then told her he would be right back. She sat in her bed too lazy to move. She was not sure what time she had fallen asleep. Kisses to her forehead were what woke her minutes later, and she smiled.

"Mmm. I thought you had ditched me," Mary whispered to him as she rolled onto her back.

"You have made that near impossible," he whispered into her hair. "I do believe I have found paradise here with you."

Mary loved the sound of that.

He lay next to her, tracing the contours of her face with his finger. He ran his thumb across her lips and followed with his lips. He ran his fingers down the length of her arms, interlacing their fingers before pulling her into him and massaging her scalp. She fit perfectly against his body as if she had been made for him.

"I really love you," he said, breaking contact and easing her onto her side to look at him.

She turned her face to his, wanting to say something but not finding the words.

"You are beautiful," she whispered, trailing her fingers across his lips and behind his head to bring him in for a hug.

"I think you upped and lost your ability to see. You are the most beautiful thing in this community."

She rubbed her nose against his momentarily, wondering again how they got there, but chose to respond differently. "Yes, I am."

Mary had found in this place and time, a man with whom she could be herself. She reveled in the strong presence of him and vowed to support him through all the perils of the job he had to do. She fell asleep feeling protected and for the moment loved and wanted. She wanted to tell him that, but sleep overcame her and all she could do was kiss his firm chest, wrap her arms around him and hope that he read the message in her gesture.

"Sweet dreams," he whispered as he kissed the top of her head and gently rubbed her bulging belly. She threw her legs possessively across his and fell asleep.

A New Life

Nearly five months later, Mary was waddling along beneath the girth of the extra human rolling about inside her.

"Do you think it will be a boy?" Michael asked her one day as she rested beneath the almond tree while the children played.

"I do not know, but it would be nice to give little Able a sister to take care of," she said with a smile.

They looked over to where the youngster in question was busy helping one of the girls his age to tie her shoelaces. He had just learnt how to do just that, and he offered to do it for everyone he saw in need of the service.

"He would like that," Michael said, but his voice was distracted. She followed his gaze, which was focused on the bishop's granddaughter, a beautiful redhead who had caught the eyes of many of the young boys.

"Have you asked her out yet?" she asked, watching him blush at being caught in the act of admiration.

He shook his head. "She would never hang out with me," he said, joking.

"You won't know if you don't ask," she told the ten-year-old. It couldn't be dating now. They were too young for that, but friends at least, was something they could work on.

"She just won't," he added, and she decided that she wouldn't push him on it.

It was a tune that rang so true to her own story as she looked across the open field to the man who had stolen her heart.

His name was Amos. She had always loved the way it sounded—a sacred whisper on her lips. She watched him in the park as he played with the young Able and the other youngsters from the community, in whose upbringing he had placed a keen interest. She could see the muscles rippling in his shoulders beneath the thin fabric of his summer shirt, his cropped hair bouncing as he ran across the grass barefooted with the young ones behind him.

He was beautiful. He had come alive. He had changed so much since she had come here, and she loved the change. It gave her what she always dreamt of, a family to call her own and a husband who understood that her past decisions did not mean she was less deserving of his love. For the first time in a very long time, she thought of this community and the place where they had all come from. She thought of the fact that she had thought love had given up on her and that she was doomed to spend the rest of her life alone and then realized that at no point in time did she ever envision her life with this much warmth and laughter. She would have it no other way. She had felt love and she knew it to be true but she still worried that one day he might wake up and decide that she was not what he wanted after all. These were insecurities placed inside her through Bryan's decision to leave her for the Englisch world. He had scarred her heart, but looking at Amos, she realized that she had nothing to fear.

"Come play, Mama." Little Able tugged at her arm and pulled at her frock. He had taken to calling her Mama, and Ruth he called Mamm. Neither woman minded in the least. Amos was Papa and Samuel was Daed. They accepted their new names with love.

She would have loved to play, but his baby sibling growing like a weed inside her sapped all the energy she had. She pulled him into her arms and tickled him so hard that all he wanted to do was to get away from her. He ran with hiccups back to the group and she settled back on her arm, using the other to lovingly caress the life inside her. She was excited and she intended to enjoy every bit of the coming months.

"No running about for you today?" Amos said, coming to sit beside her. She smiled at him and shook her head. It was a pensive Sunday for her.

He took her hand and kissed the back of it, and she turned to look at him. His every breath pulled her into him. She felt the warmth in his eyes every time he looked at her and she knew she was blessed. He snapped his finger in front of her before bending to kiss her.

"Let it all go and come back to me." He smiled at her.

The children whistled and he laughed as he kissed her forehead, but she wanted to send them all to bed.

She stared at him and smiled. The sun reflecting from his eyes danced as he mocked her. She had fallen deeper in love with him over the past weeks. He had treated her with nothing but kindness and consideration and opened every aspect of his life to her. She had learnt to hold no secrets from him and through his eyes she saw herself in a different light.

"I love you, Amos Yoder," she whispered, resting her forehead against his chin.

"And you are forever mine." He kissed her forehead, sealing that promise for a lifetime.

When she went into labor, she had forgotten that bearing a child could bring her this much pain. She was certain she would die from it.

Mary screamed in pain, unable to bear the way her body stretched to unfathomable lengths.

"Almost there, Mary, just a little bit more," the midwife urged.

Mary screamed in pain. "I can't! I just can't!" The pain of childbirth had her swooning in and out of consciousness, she just wanted the child out of her.

"One more push," the midwife urged, and Mary mustered all she could, screaming in pain as she tried to evict the tiny human from her womb.

The small wailing of a baby moments later as she felt the child slip from her was enough to tell her the pain had been worth it.

"It's a girl!" the midwife called to her joyously.

She laughed, weary with the exhaustion of having given birth but strong with the need to see her child before she slept. "Where is she? Where is she?"

Wrapped in cloth and wet form the hurried wash, the baby was placed in her mother's arms as her father came bursting through the doors.

"Mary!" he rushed to her side. "Mary!"

She smiled up at him as he gave her a kiss, and a tear slipped from his eye as he looked down at the baby she held in her arms.

"Isn't she beautiful?" Mary asked as the baby stopped crying and began to coo in her arms.

"Yes," Amos said, running his fingers over the face of his newborn child. "Yes, she is just as beautiful as her mamm."

He placed a kiss on her forehead, and she fell asleep with the knowledge that she had found love and it had started her life anew. She looked forward to the years of happiness to come and knew that it would be all she hoped for and more than she could ever imagine.

"We will call her Anna," he said. She smiled up at him and nodded. That would be perfect. As was everything else around her.

A new chapter

A year after little Able had been rescued from the mentally disturbed Ellen, all was well in the world in which Mary and Amos Yoder and their community lived. Little baby Anna Yoder was quite simply enthralled by her big brother, Able. Able, for his part, was more than likely the most astute and attentive big brother ever to grace Gott's good earth. He took his role very seriously indeed, and his adopted Mamm and Daed, Ruth and Samuel, allowed him liberty to interact with Anna as such as freely as was reasonable. Of course, as Anna's parents and Able's biological Mamm, Mary and Amos were as proud as can be of Able and the manner in which he took care of his schweschder. The love the two kinners Mary had birthed had for one another was as palpable as could be imagined. Baby Anna could contentedly stare at Able for the longest time, the awe plain to see on her cherub-like baby face. It was not as if big brother Able did not take full advantage of playing to his audience, however. Able loved that his schweschder adored him, and he adored her in equal measure. He had donned the cape of protector and adorer, and he wore it well and with pride. Yes, he knew full well that pride was looked down upon in the Amish community. That was the reason behind him checking with the bishop one Sunday after home church, whereupon the bishop had assured him that Gott smiled down upon the pride he had in little Anna.

Able was apprehensive about returning to the school at which his captor, Ellen, had taught before abducting him and telling him that his adopted parents no longer wanted him. It was therefore a blessing that Mary had been given the position of full-time teacher at the little school before she was blessed with the arrival of little Anna. Her assuring presence at the school before leaving to have her baby was the only prompter for getting Able to return to classes. Since her absence after Anna's birth, he often wandered off on the way to school, and sometimes failed to arrive at school at all in the mornings. Since he had gone missing before, it was only natural that all who loved him were overly concerned whenever this happened. Many were the times that an informal search party was thrown together to find the lost little Amish boy when he failed to turn up at the classroom.

It was a bright summer morning without a cloud in the sky, and Able did not look forward to spending the morning in the classroom without Mary. He was almost seven, and he should not have to go to school any more if he didn't want to. He could read as well as the next kinner, and he could add and subtract numbers. More importantly, he could help shod a plow horse; he could brush down the buggy horses; he could fork hay into the horses' stalls at feed times; he could milk the cows—all seven of the ones Samuel kept on their farm; and he could read his Bible with Samuel before bedtime. More importantly still, he could take care of all his schweschder's needs and help Mary to change, dress, feed and bathe her and keep her company whenever her mamm had the need to leave her unattended for a few minutes. What purpose did it serve for him to have to sit in a stuffy classroom with all the other kinners who might not have important matters to attend to such that he had?

He would spend the morning down at the creek where Mary had often told him the rainbows and unicorns would gather when no one was about. He imagined that this was where magic happened, where mushrooms and brightly patterned toadstools burst forth from the mossy, shaded areas and little forest creatures peeked out ahead of his arrival to watch him watching them as he walked. One day he planned on being stealthy enough to surprise the gathered unicorns and rainbows beside the creek. He imagined peering at them from a well-thought-out hiding spot and seeing the fantastical creatures and the beautifully colored rainbows doing whatever it was they gathered here to achieve.

He had interrupted Samuel once while he was reading to him about the animals Noah rescued on the impossibly massive wooden boat the people all laughed at him for building. Samuel put the Bible down to listen to his sonn, who asked why it was that the unicorns were not mentioned in the Bible story about the ark. Able had seen how his daed had tried not to smile at the question.

"I can't assume to know more than what is written

in the pages of the Bible, my sonn. Gott knows what is important for His sons and daughters to know," Samuel had explained. "I can only tell you what I think might be the reason. Would you like to hear?"

"Jah, Daed. Please tell me what you think is the reason Gott might have for leaving out such an important creature."

Samuel was not aware of the significance of the unicorn in both Mary and her biological sonn Able's life, or he might have suggested Able speak with Mary about Noah's reasons.

"I think that only some special people see unicorns as being real. Maybe the ark story does not want to take away the special nature of the unicorn by talking of them to people who don't already believe in them," Samuel offered as explanation. "It is true that some people can only believe in what they can see. Anything that cannot be seen or touched or smelled does not exist to these people."

"I cannot see Gott," Able sighed, shrugging his shoulders. "Do people who don't think unicorns are real also not believe that Gott is real?"

This discussion was becoming complicated to Samuel's mind and he wondered at the innocent mind of a kinner that could think up questions that were so hard for a parent to answer.

"Gott is indeed not real to some people. It is the way it is." Samuel shrugged too.

At this, Able took Samuel's hand and looked up at him. "Does Ellen believe, do you think, Daed?"

Samuel knew that his reaction to the question was not good. His body had stiffened involuntarily when his

beloved sonn mentioned the fraa who had stolen Able
and told him that he and Ruth no longer wanted him.
That incident had been very traumatic for the kind and
for all who loved Able, especially Ruth and Mary and
he himself. Never before or since had Samuel prayed
so vehemently to Gott for His blessing and grace to be
poured upon Able so that he might be returned safely
to Ruth and him. Gott had thankfully seen fit to answer
Samuel's prayers, and the little boy had not mentioned
Ellen since seeing her removed by the police after he
had successfully escaped almost two years before.

"I know she always did believe in Gott. Ellen was
always a Gott-fearing fraa. I can't say much more
about her than that, and that she loved her husband
very dearly. Maybe losing him caused her to behave in
a way that was not entirely as she might have had he
not been taken in death." Samuel patted his sonn's little
hand and smiled.

Able smiled back up at his daed and asked, "Will
you be reading to me how Noah sailed the ark for one
hundred and fifty days with all the animals on board?"

Samuel was surprised at the boy's knowledge of the
details, "How many days, Able?"

"One hundred and fifty. That is what Mamm Mary
told us when she was teaching at the school. Why can
she not come back to teach us now that Gott has blessed
her and Amos with baby Anna, my schweschder?"

"Well, don't you think that it is a gut thing that Anna
has her home to take care of her while she is still so
small and unable to do all those things for herself?"

"I think that it would be a gut thing for her to bring
Anna with her to the school when she teaches us. That

way I will be able to look after Anna if she needs me, and the kinners will all be very happy having Mary as a teacher."

Samuel smiled. "You are indeed a very clever young mann, Able."

But for the moment, Able had given up peering out from his clever hiding spot beside the creek and was stepping over the slippery boulders which poked out above the softly flowing water of the rippling river in the creek. He must have missed the rainbows and the unicorns yet again, he thought to himself as he focused on stepping carefully from one boulder to the next. At last he reached the grouping of large boulders near the center of the widest part of the river. This was where Able would lie listening to the music of the flowing river, absorbing the warmth of the sun. It wasn't long before he drifted off to sleep, surrounded by the soothing waters. His last thought before falling asleep was whether this was also Noah and his family's experience for those one hundred and fifty days on board the ark with only the animals for company.

Ellen

Seeing all the people she had known all her life watching her being manhandled by the police officers was very confusing to Ellen Hertzler. She was photographed and her fingerprints were taken and filed at the police station, and then she was locked in a holding cell with the most ungodly women imaginable. What was becoming of the world that she would be treated in such a way, had been her main thought throughout that day and the next.

She woke up the next morning still in the holding cell. She remembered being provided with a scratchy blanket and a pillow the night before. She also remembered having no alternative but to stretch out on the concrete floor along with the other women, to get whatever sleep she could, hampered as it was by all the noises to which she was so unaccustomed. Her mind was a haze and she could not understand why it was that she was not at home where she belonged. When she asked the guard who passed by later that morning, the women sharing her cell only laughed at the question, and the guard paid her no attention whatsoever. It was not long after that a different guard opened the cell door and called for Ellen to step out of the cell into the corridor. She did so and waited for the guard to lock the cell behind her, before following her along the stark corridor and out another door which the guard also had to unlock before they could proceed. She found herself in a police transport vehicle which, after a confusing drive, parked in an underground parking facility, where she was taken from the back, handcuffed and shackled at the ankles. What could she possibly have done to deserve this treatment?

From the parking lot, she was locked in what she imagined must be some form of interview room. But why was she shackled and locked away wherever she went? And who were all these people? Where was her bishop and all the people from her community? She was left alone in the locked room which boasted only a table and two chairs. Not long after, the door was unlocked and Jonathan stepped into the room, bending to enter the doorway. He was accompanied by a man with a black leather briefcase. A policeman stepped in behind the two men and placed a third chair in the room before leaving them alone in the room, closing the door behind himself and taking up position outside the door. Ellen was very pleased to see Jonathan, the unmarried community elder with whom she had attended school as a young girl. Jonathan looked into her eyes and took the chair opposite her while the strange man in the suit and tie seated himself on the chair near the door. Jonathan's eyes did not leave her face as the strange man opened his briefcase and removed a gray file which he placed still closed on his lap.

"Ellen Hertzler, are you being treated well enough?" Johnathan asked.

Ellen could not help but think what a strange question that was for Johnathan to ask her. She shrugged and dropped her eyes to her hands in her lap.

"Do you know where you are?" he persisted.

"I don't know. I was brought here in a van. The van was parked in a lot underground. I could not see out of the van while we were driving and I saw nothing but the concrete pillars of the underground parking, and the cars parked in the lot." She shrugged again and looked up at the mann she had known since childhood.

"Do you know why you are here?" Johnathan asked, looking at the man seated in the room with them.

Ellen shrugged again but remained silent.

"Ellen Hertzler," Johnathan prompted gently, "This is Shaun Barnett." The man nodded to her. "He is a lawyer. He will be asking you questions about all that the police are charging you with. Do you understand?"

Ellen dared to look into the face of the strange man who was apparently to represent her because she had charges laid against her. "I don't understand," she said simply, and looked away from the man who was Shaun Barnett.

Shaun spoke then. "Mrs. Hertzler," he said as he swopped chairs with Johnathan, and opened the file on the table between her and him. "The state has charged that you kidnapped one Able Beiler, a five-year old child from the Amish community in which you reside.

We need to know whether you accept these charges or whether you will be pleading not guilty in court."

"Ruth and Samuel Beiler have each other. They did not deserve to be gifted the boy by that whore Mary Lapp. Able was meant to be my child, not theirs. It was all a mistake," Ellen barked, her eyes blazing with all the intensity of the injustice of the situation.

The lawyer looked at Johnathan, who shook his head very slightly. "Do you need anything, Ellen?" Johnathan asked the suddenly animated woman.

She looked at him with no sign of understanding the circumstances in which she was embroiled, and simply shook her head from side to side. As if the movement had triggered a recollection, she looked up at Johnathan and said, "I don't have my prayer kapp. Do you know who has my prayer kapp?"

Johnathan's dismay was clear to see on his face as he shook his head in answer. "I don't know, Ellen. I don't think you are permitted to wear your kapp in here."

"But I am to wear my prayer kapp at all times that I am in company. It preserves my modesty," she explained in an earnest tone.

When neither mann responded, she added, "The scriptures tell us 'In like manner also, that women adorn themselves in modest apparel, with shamefacedness and sobriety; not with broided hair, or gold, or pearls, or costly array'."

Johnathan looked enquiringly at the lawyer and raised his eyebrows to accentuate his need for an answer. Shaun cleared his throat, his discomfort more than evident.

"Mrs. Hertzler, it is for your own protection that the

bonnet has been taken from you. Rest assured that is being kept safe for you and will be returned when the time is right," he offered by way of explanation.

The men seemed visibly relieved that she appeared to have accepted the explanation. "Mrs. Hertzler, we have arranged for you to be seen by a doctor. Please be assured that this is for your own good and that it is in your own best interests that you cooperate with him or her and answer all the questions put to you in the most helpful way and as fully and comprehensibly as you possibly can," the lawyer continued. When Ellen failed to respond, he asked, "Do you understand, Mrs. Hertzler?"

"I don't think that I am in need of medical attention, denke, Mister…" She faltered momentarily, shook her head as if to clear cobwebs from within, and continued, "I am sorry, I am not good with remembering names. I think that all I need now is to be allowed to return to my home. Denke again. I am sure that it is almost time for me to host the Sunday home church, and I will need to get busy with the cooking and the preparation." Ellen made to get up from the chair. It was as if she had forgotten that she was shackled, and again confusion flooded the woman's features. She looked up at Johnathan as if pleading wordlessly for his help.

"Is there any way that she can go home?" Johnathan asked the lawyer in a sideways manner as if that would deter Ellen from overhearing.

"Sir, you do understand that she is facing very serious charges, and that her mental stability is also in question here? Do you honestly believe that she will be safe out in the real world, mingling with the very people she sought to harm only days ago? Did you understand what she said moments ago about the Beiler couple having the child that she believes was meant to be hers?"

Johnathan's look of resignation said all the lawyer needed to know, and the two menner stood to leave.

"Mrs. Hertzler, you will be seen by a doctor and you should do all that you can to show at this time that you understand the consequences of your actions in taking the child. Do you understand?" The lawyer attempted once again to get through to the woman who was deteriorating into an ever-increasingly pitiful creature before their very eyes.

She simply nodded, keeping her eyes downcast.

A feeling Inside

Susan Stoll opened the suspect's file and sighed heavily, swiftly transported back in time to her childhood. A life characterized by time standing still. Susan was the middle child of seven children, living a prescribed life in the incredibly conservative New York Swartzentruber Amish community, Heuvelton, near the Canadian border.

The Swartzentruber group vehemently maintained the core characterization of separating themselves from the world. By its very definition, this characterization is accentuated. Swartz is the German word meaning black, which as the most conservative color appropriately represents this Amish group. The meaning of Truber is to refrain or hold back. Comparatively speaking, the Swartzentruber group has successfully refrained from the temptations and changes evident in most other Amish communities.

She recalled boarding the Greyhound bus in 1974, helping with the younger kinners, to relocate from Holmes County, Ohio, to as far North as was possible without leaving America. Ongoing church dissension had preempted the mass move of the many Amish who were looking for available and affordable farmlands. Of course among the reasons was also the need to preserve their homogeneity and avoid the conflict surrounding their strict excommunication practices. The result was a highly conformist Amish community with more stringent ordnung rules regarding dress, appearance, traditionalism and unquestioning obedience. Noah Stoll built their new haus, assisted by the community and his kinners. The haus was as plain as was possible, without carpeting or even linoleum flooring, upholstered furniture or indoor toilets. Oil lamps were the only source of unnatural light. Gas and battery-powered lamps were strictly forbidden, as were battery-operated calculators. The kitchen had a dry sink and a wood-burning oven which served as a water heater, and a producer of heat in the winter and hot meals and baked goods for the family every day of the year, winter or summer, fall or spring.

Susan had three older bruders, a younger bruder and two younger schweschders. As the oldest girl, she was tasked with quilting to bring in an income. The fraa quilt much more up North than most other communities, and the majority of the quilts made are sold outside of the community. Despite not being permitted to advertise their products, the Heuvelton women managed a prosperous trade in their beautiful works. Susan was among the best quilters, which was of course never acknowledged since pride was not tolerated. Modesty was the epitome of Amish existence, and accomplishments were expected rather than rewarded.

The Bible promotes being equally yoked and to be of

likeness, and Susan's community therefore believed it would not be a sound Biblical coaching to marry outside their group. Swartzentrubers married only Swartzentrubers. It was this ordnung prerequisite that eventually proved to be the straw that broke the proverbial back. Susan had more than just a thirst for knowledge and a love of learning. She had the objectionable trait of desiring freedom of choice. She once challenged an elder with the question that if Gott separated the mann from the animals by giving mann freedom of choice, why did mann choose to shackle themselves by laws and the ordnung. It was a controversial question and she was severely admonished and punished by look and word for a very long time after. It is difficult to determine whether her thirst for knowledge caused her to take up the town librarian's offer to use the reference section or whether the many months spent in the library caused the thirst in the first place. Whichever was the case, the librarian, Katie, was instrumental in her learning to use the computer, and enrolling in a home-schooling system which earned her a first-class education. Her results earned her a full scholarship to study Psychology at a New York university.

She would never be allowed to communicate with her family again if she chose to take up the scholarship rather than marry the Amish mann who had asked to court her and settle into a traditional Amish life after being baptized into the church. She made her unpopular decision and was summarily shunned and banished from the community. It was a sad day when her family members all physically turned their backs on her, as she left the haus for the final time, her small bag in hand and her Bible tucked under her arm.

Four years later she earned her bachelor degree cum laude, top of the class, and walked into the master's degree program also with a full scholarship. After two more years, she started her PhD, and four years later she was Doctor Susan Stoll, Forensic Psychologist for New York State. The years rolled by and she became the most experienced and sought-after forensic psychologist for criminal cases and court testimonies. Ellen Hertzler's case was not her first Amish-related litigation.

When she saw the broken woman in the interview room, her heart went out to her. She knew what it was like to lose the support of the people with whom she was supposed to relate. She also knew that Ellen would have known only the people within her Amish community, the very like-minded people who had not asked after her since her incarceration or attempted to visit her or reach out to her in any way. Ellen Hertzler was an island, and no man could survive as an island. She was drifting without the anchorage she required now more than ever: that of the Christian support of her own. Of course Susan was not unsympathetic of the perspective of the community involved. Ellen had stolen a much-loved young member of the community; a boy who had been lovingly adopted by a couple and then reabsorbed into the arms of his biological mother, who could not bear a life without her rightful, Gott-given sonn. He was uniquely loved by both an adoptive family and his extended biological family. And Ellen had wanted to sever that bond of blood and love by trying to convince the boy that he was no longer wanted or loved by anyone but her. What a cruel affliction to throw upon a young boy.

It took only two visits with Ellen to diagnose her as suffering from Persecution Complex, an irrational and obsessive feeling of being the object of collective hostility and harassment.

"Ellen, would you like to tell me about Able?" Susan prompted.

"I must have my kapp before I can talk to anyone. This is not proper."

"What is not proper, Ellen?"

"For me not to display the modesty that is proper for a fraa. What would my husband think?"

"Where is your husband?" the doctor persevered.

"He…" Ellen mumbled incoherently, shaking her head from side to side as if to dislodge a memory or deny a voice inside her own head.

"Do you remember when last you saw your husband? Where were you, Ellen?"

Ellen looked up and the clouds lifted from her eyes. "He was in our living room in our haus."

"Can you tell me what he was doing?"

"I dressed him in a white vest, white pants and white shirt. Samuel Fisher brought the coffin in after I had washed him and he was lying in the coffin after I dressed him."

When Ellen paused, Susan asked, "You washed and dressed him? By yourself?" knowing full well that Ellen had not been in the right frame of mind after losing her husband to have done so, and that Ruth Beiler had offered to do it on her behalf.

* * *

"Jah. I did it. He was my husband. Samuel and his three sons had carried all our furniture from the living room and placed them in the barn. That's what we do, you know, before the people come to view the body for the first time after a death." Ellen looked up to explain to Susan, who nodded appropriately to encourage her to continue.

"Jah and so Mr. Hertzler was lying in the open coffin that Samuel Fisher built and carried in to the living room after he and his sonns had cleared..." She shook her head again. "I have told you this. I am sorry. When the room was fit for the viewing, the people started to come. We held a small service in our haus, which was when the second viewing took place. At the funeral itself. You see, our community has never seen the need for a formal church. It is unnecessary since we can congregate for services in the homes of the community members or in the schoolhaus. The third viewing was at the graveside at the lonely little burial site on the hill near to the forest. And after that Mr. Hertzler's body was interred and the final service was held."

"Ellen, what was your husband's name?" Susan prompted, finding it odd even for an Amish widow to refer to her husband as Mr. Hertzler rather than by a term of endearment or his Christian name.

Ellen's face verily flushed an angry red, and she became animate for the first time since Susan's visits. "You did not know him! He was *my* husband!"

"And you loved him very much and you miss him?"

"We only had each another in the world." Her face

hardened. "Gott did not see His way to give us kinners. And when He planted the seed in the wayward Mary Lapp, Gott meant for *us* to have the baby. But evil interceded and Ruth and Samuel got the boppli. They found him on their doorstep, did you know? It was at night. Late at night. In the cold," she blurted accusingly.

Susan nodded.

Ellen suddenly looked about her, a terrified look blanketing her features. "I must go now. They don't want me here anymore."

"Who does not want you here, Ellen?"

"No one wants me around. Anywhere. No one," her voice trailed off hopelessly. "They took my boppli and now they don't want me around."

When she erupted into hysteric tears and began to fling her upper body from side to side, the guards entered the room and she was removed, leaving Susan alone in the desolate room, designed to intimidate.

The Yoder haus

The community had moved on with their lives. They were a stoic people, and gossip and speculation were not their way. Although the police kept them updated on the case against Ellen, no one spoke of it in public. Mary and Amos always discussed the case after hearing from the police, but only in the privacy of their haus and never in the company of others. The policeman had just left their haus after accepting a cup of kaffe and a sugar cookie on their porch, enjoying the later afternoon summer sun. He had said that Ellen was being seen by a forensic psychologist who would determine whether she was mentally fit to stand trial. It was indeed a sad turn of events which had disrupted not only their lives, but the entire tight-knit community. Little Able still suffered nightmares, although very rarely now. It hardly seemed fair that such a loved young boy would have to suffer such an unnecessary experience. Why would Gott subject them all to this? She knew that it was not for her to question His ways and His decision. She knew that her faith was strong, but she would nonetheless have liked to know the reasons behind this path they had all been led down. Where would it lead? What would be found at the end of it? How could it ever be of any benefit to Able to have been removed from those he loved and to be told that he was no longer loved or wanted? She shook her head, unable to make sense of any of it.

She could not have her days taken up with thoughts of Ellen Hertzler, though. She had a baby girl to care for and a haus and husband to see to, not to mention the summer vegetable garden and the small orchard that had to be harvested. Once she had done that, she could make the fruit preserve she had become famous for, to sell at the farmers market coming up. She chased Amos out to the barn to finish his chores, asking him to take Anna with him, and she got up off the rocker on the porch to get her tasks done.

Anna loved to tag along with her daed while he tackled his daily tasks. She especially loved working with the horses, with who she seemed to have an unnatural connection. As Mary watched the two people she loved the most in the world, she wondered whether her baby girl could perhaps understand the horses, and vice versa. She had heard mention of a horse whisperer in the Montana area some years ago who had just such an affiliation with the stately creatures. She would not be sad for her daughter to have this gift too. But she could not procrastinate any longer; the fruits of her labor would not be harvested without yet more of her labor going into it.

It was some months before they heard from the police again. Ellen Hertzler had been determined unfit to stand trial. She was being held in an inpatient psychiatric unit in which two characterizations of patients accused of crimes are made: Acutes are those whom the doctors regard as still sick enough to be fixed; and Chronics are in for good without hope of curing or release. Ellen hung in the balance between the two, pending further treatment and diagnosis. Was the rest of her life to be lived in some fearful and mystifying state of limbo?

Hopeless

Prison of any sort is not designed to be enjoyable. But for the Amish it is so far removed from the norm that they have a harder time than most adapting to the change that it demands.

Ellen was not permitted to wear the plain clothes she was accustomed to. For the first time in her life, she spent day in and day out in long pants. Jumpsuits. Somber washed-out gray in color. Much like the coveralls that the menner wore when they worked their farms back in the communities. Only these had zippers. And she was not permitted to wear a kapp or head covering of any sort, because she was on suicide watch. Of course, they were all on suicide watch in here. Not one of the people she shared her life and space with in this new life that was now her reality and her existence was of stable mind. They were all capable of the unimaginable. This hell was where the unimaginable was expected and where measures were constantly in place to make it as difficult as possible for the inmates, or patients as they were kindly referred to—political correctness being a prerequisite in an abnormal world—to act out on their impulses or madness.

Correctional facilities across the country struggle with now being the nation's de facto mental healthcare providers. Since the deinstitutionalization of state mental hospitals in the mid-twentieth century, which had become renowned as places of widespread cruelty and inhumanity, this may not be the worst that could have happened for the mentally inept criminals. But the fact remains that the inpatient psychiatric units within the prison system are despairingly ill-equipped to handle the task of managing tens of thousands of inmates afflicted with a variety of classified and recognized mental disorders.

Ellen was therefore fortunate beyond measure that Doctor Susan Stoll made the decision to maintain a professional interest in her and her case, even after she had recommended Ellen be considered mentally incapable of standing trial for the kidnapping of little Able Beiler. The correctional system allowed for Susan to see Ellen whenever she felt it necessary to do so. Over the first year of Ellen's incarceration, she was often placed in solitary confinement because of her unnatural inclination to believe beyond a doubt that one or more of her fellow inmates was out to get her for some imagined reason or another. Of course this imagined threat to her safety and security was as real to Ellen's mind as it would be to any one of us walking the streets of a notoriously crime-ridden inner city area in the small hours of the morning. It was believed that solitary confinement was the safest place for her. Paradoxically it usually served to increase her delusional paranoia for whatever reason. When Susan visited only to learn that Ellen was once again assigned to solitary, Susan was livid beyond explanation. She moved to have her relocated to a unit more suited to her particular disposition. After almost a year, the courts granted permission for Ellen to be moved to a minimum-security psychiatric unit. Despite being accused of a serious felony offense, typically carrying a prison sentence of twenty years or more, depending on the circumstances of the case, Susan's arguments won the courts over. Ellen was assigned work duties in the prison's kitchen gardens, and this had a phenomenally positive impact on both her physical well-being and her state of mind. She still chose to isolate herself from the other inmates and prison staff. She would spend a great deal of her time reading her Bible and cleaning her small cubicle which had only her fixed bed, a cabinet and a shelf. She hated having to share the bathroom facilities, being that her beliefs demanded immense modesty. She hated being subjected to television. She never received visitors, except for Doctor Susan Stoll, who popped in unannounced and without forewarning, which was unusual in itself.

During her fourth year behind bars, so to say, permission was given for Doctor Stoll to take Ellen to a psychiatric unit in the city to take part in a state study on mental illness within the various types of correctional services departments in the State. The study progressed so well that Ellen became a standard member of the 'team', and she was often transported from the prison to the hospital under prison guard. This procedure became so standard that the guards eventually became lax in their duties and Ellen was able to walk out of the psychiatric hospital wearing the clothes of a young intern she had knocked unconscious, undressed and stuffed in the shower cubicle of a wing of the hospital currently undergoing refurbishment.

Where is Anna?

It was left up to the bishop to decide what was to be done with the property that had belonged to the Hertzlers. After many months of deliberation, it was decided that the farm would be hired out within the Amish community, and the proceeds kept in safekeeping for Ellen Hertzler. A young couple recently married and blessed with a boppli hired the farm. The powers that be were contacted within the correctional system, and it was found that Ellen would benefit from having funds paid into her commissary. These funds she could use to purchase whatever the prison provided for sale to the prisoners.

Peter and Sissy Horst had seen the availability of the Hertzler property as a sign from Gott, being that the timing was perfectly aligned with their need. The two had been too young to know the dastardly details of the Hertzler/Beiler matter, and so they were in no way daunted by living in the haus last occupied by the mad kidnapper, Ellen Hertzler. Life had gone on as normal outside of the small circle of families directly affected by Ellen's actions so many years before. Fortunately the Hertzler haus had been maintained by concerned neighbors during the time that it had stood vacant, and so the couple were able to move in after just refreshing the paint and sweeping out the rooms. Just three months after taking up residence, Sissy found out that they could expect the arrival of their first boppli before fall. Peter had been gifted dairy cows by his daed, and the little dairy on the farm was soon producing sufficiently to see to the needs of the haus and the couple. Peter was carving a cradle in the secrecy of the barn, in anticipation of the arrival of their boppli, during every spare moment, unbeknownst to Sissy whose girth was increasing by the day to accommodate the growing child.

The women of the region had arranged a tea for her to celebrate the coming of the child, during her last trimester of pregnancy. Peter had taken the opportunity to ensconce himself in the barn where he worked diligently on the finishing touches of the cradle. While Sissy exclaimed excitedly over each handmade gift from the women of the community, Peter was content to move about the barn on the business of doing what any expectant daed would be doing.

Amos had dropped Mary off at the Beiler house where young Sissy's tea was being hosted. He had volunteered to take Able and Anna with him to visit Peter at the erstwhile Hertzler haus to give the women opportunity to enjoy the gathering without having to worry about the kinners. Able was in his final year of school, being almost thirteen, and little Anna had not yet started attending classes, although she did accompany her mamm to the schoolhaus, where she taught the kinners their lessons on every school day. The two kinners were excited to spend the day doing menner tasks with Amos and Peter. They had not been looking forward to being cooped up in the Beiler house while the women chatted and drank tea and ate baked goods together.

Peter had the unsettling sensation of eyes on him, which was unreasonable to his own mind but nonetheless unshakable. He moved about the barn easily, comfortable in the space that had become his own over the months. When he heard the buggy roll into his yard, he put the chisels back in their receptacle and hid the cradle beneath the canvas square before leaving the confines of the barn. Stepping outside he was momentarily blinded by the bright summer sun which was high in the sky. Shielding his eyes until they adjusted to the sunlight, he was pleased to see Amos and the two kinners riding the buggy into his yard. He removed his hat and slapped it against the sawdust-covered coverall leg, displacing the dust, which danced in the sun's rays as he waited for the three to climb down from the buggy. They unhitched the horse and led it into the barn once it was understood that Amos would be visiting for a while. Peter had been expecting Amos, it having been decided some weeks before that Amos would help with the final touches of the boppli's nursery in the haus. Sissy and Peter had cleared the upstairs bedroom next to theirs of furniture and painted it out. Sissy had sewed the drapes for the window, and Peter had promised they would go into town to buy a cupboard for the baby's room just as soon as they had the chance. This had just been the smallest of white lies though, since Peter had already commissioned his childhood friend and the best carpenter in the community to craft them a specially designed cupboard. When it was completed, it had been secreted into the barn, taking its temporary position beside the cradle under the canvas square. The plan was for Amos and Able to help carry the cupboard and the cradle upstairs to the room, where they would also hang the newly sewn drapes.

Able was delighted to be instrumental in the surprise, and he and little Anna headed up the stairs to the kitchen door, leaving the menner behind in the yard. Together they swung the door open and swept inside, rushing up the stairs to the bedrooms. Able took his role very seriously and he stooped down beside Anna in the empty nursery room to explain that this was to be the room for a new boppli, and that she was to tell no one of what they would be doing there on this day. Anna nodded earnestly and followed her big bruder down the stairs, out the kitchen, across the yard and into the barn where the two menner were already busy finishing off the cradle.

It was not long before Amos was carrying the cradle up the stairs to the porch, with Peter and Able following behind, carrying the cupboard. Amos positioned the cradle on his hip to open the swing door into the kitchen, stepped inside and held the door open with his foot for the two to carry the cupboard inside. Amos let the door slide closed after the cupboard was carried inside, and the three marched in procession up the stairs to the nursery room, carrying their cargo. It had already been decided where the furniture would be placed, and the menner stood back to admire the now furnished room before Able gathered the curtains up and they got them hung in the window. Able drew the curtains and then opened them again to test the placement, and he could have sworn that he saw a movement beyond the barn. On second look however he had to concede that the light must have been playing tricks on his eyes, as there was nothing to see now.

"Where's Anna?" Able asked in passing.

Amos stopped repositioning the cradle to look about the room for his dochder. "She was here. Wasn't she?"

No one could recall whether she had followed them into the room, or even whether she had accompanied them into the haus. She might have been distracted in the barn, for all they could determine. Able suddenly had a chill up his spine and he darted out the room and down the stairs. He shot out the kitchen door and down the porch stairs, across the grassed yard and into the barn. It was empty. Then he remembered the movement he thought he had imagined early from the boppli's room window. He turned and ran for the barn door, passing Peter and Amos in the doorway.

"Able! What is it?" Amos asked, trying to suppress the panic rising in his voice.

"I think I saw Anna in the field behind the barn just now from the window upstairs."

Amos looked up to the window to determine the area visible from that vantage point, and then followed Able who was running around the barn.

Once they were behind the barn and had a clear view of the fields, Able decided the likely direction of the movement. The three menner ran in the direction of Mr.

Raber's orchards. Amos thought to shout to Peter to get to the community phone and get the police there, telling him to be sure to tell them that Ellen Hertzlcr had likely taken their dochder, Anna Yoder.

Home is where the heart is

Ellen had made her way to the only place she had ever known as home. Her progress was slow and deliberate. The police had put out an immediate alert for her and roadblocks had quickly sprung up all over the state as soon as her presence in the hospital was missed. Ellen's resourcefulness was underappreciated, however, and she evaded all attempts to find her. It took her ten days to reach 'home', which was also under the watchful eye of the law, who expected her to turn up there at any time. They were however not looking for a short-haired blond man, wearing Amish coveralls and men's boots. Her disguise was ingenious, and she slipped through all obstacles to her returning home.

She was beyond exhausted when she eventually reached the road outside of the city. She had a long way to go before she reached her Amish community. But before she could go any further, she had things to do. She stole a couple of pairs of men's coveralls from a washing line, and a pair of men's boots from the porch of another haus along the route before lifting a pair of shears from a barn. After some days and nights on the road, sleeping under bridges and eating whatever food she could come by, she at last reached the pond near the road to her haus. Here she had sat beside the pond and waited for her reflection to clear in the rippling water. She lifted the shears in her right hand, taking her long hair in the other. And she severed the handful of hair in one manipulation of the blades. She did it over and over again until her long hair lay on the ground before her. She got up off the ground and kicked the tresses into the water, where they floated on the water, across the pond. She walked away to remove her clothes in the reeds. When she stepped back into the open, she was wearing the coveralls and the boots. Her transformation was complete. She ran her hands down the legs of the coveralls and turned in the direction of home.

Home was a sight for sore eyes. She could not remember how long it had been since she had been in her haus. She was so looking forward to sitting on her porch with a hot cup of kaffe and a slice of homemade bread, spread thick with Missy Stoltzfus's homemade creamy butter. And maybe there would still be sugar cookies left in the cookie bin above the work counter in the kitchen. She could not remember when last she had baked cookies, but it could not have been too long ago for them to already be finished.

It took her a while to get accustomed to walking in the men's boots. By the time she turned into the gateway to the haus, she was walking as if she had always worn the boots. She could hear a sound coming from the barn. Maybe her husband was working in there? She would not disturb him just yet. She climbed the stairs to the kitchen door and swung the swing door open. She stepped into the familiar room and took a deep, cleansing breath, savoring the smell of home. Why could she not smell the Brut aftershave her husband sometimes wore? She shrugged and put the kettle onto the hot stove plate before setting a up on the counter and spooning kaffe into the kaffe pot. She waited for the kettle to boil, looking about her at the haus. Where had that chair come from? Was her husband surprising her with new furniture? He was so good to her. If only she had been able to give him the blessing of a boppli. But it was not too late. Gott's timing was not the same as mann's. And Gott's timing was perfect and not to be questioned. Her thoughts were interrupted by the whistling of the boiling kettle. She lifted the kettle from the plate, remembering to use the cloth so as not to burn her hand on the hot handle. She poured the steaming water into the kaffe pot, replaced the kettle on the sideboard, and fitted the lid onto the kaffe pot. Once the grounds were properly infused, she poured herself a cup of kaffe and topped the cup up with fresh cream from the ice box in the corner. The sight of Peter's insulin medication in the ice box brought back the realization that her husband was very ill with cancer. It was as if a blanket of despair had fallen over her entire body, blocking out the warmth of gratitude to be home. She looked up from her cup, across the room to the living room, and in her mind's eye she saw her husband lying in his coffin, ready for visitation to begin. Ellen stepped out of the kitchen and walked to the living room, where in her damaged mind she now stood beside her husband's body.

Looking down at him wearing the white vest, white

shirt and white pants, she inexplicably remembered telling a lady doctor how she had dressed him for placement in the coffin. She even remembered the doctor asking her if she was certain that she was in fact the one to have washed and dressed her husband after his death. She even remembered having assured the doctor that she had been the person responsible for washing and dressing his corpse. But she had not washed or dressed him. Ruth Beiler had washed her husband. Ruth Beiler had dressed her husband in the white vest and the white shirt and the white pants. Like an ice-cold sheet of water, she remembered. Ruth Beiler had stolen her baby. Ruth Beiler and Samuel Beiler had taken the baby boy that Gott had intended for her and her husband to have.

Then the coffin disappeared, and Ellen was standing in a room furnished with items she did not recognize. Where was the coffin that Samuel Fisher had made for her husband and brought into the haus and placed in the living room which he and his sonns had cleared of furniture for the viewing of her husband's body? Where was her baby?

Then she heard the kitchen door swing open and she stooped behind the sofa as she watched a boy walking hand in hand with a little girl across the room as if he had business in the haus. Who were these intruders? Of course, this was her little girl! The boy was the one who was intended to be theirs, and because he had been taken away, he was bringing a little girl to her to take his place. Gott was gut. She watched as the two ran up the stairs. She was about to come out of her hiding place when the paranoia overwhelmed her. What if this was another trick? What if they were using her little girl to catch her? She was not as stupid as they thought she was. No one ever gave her due credit. They never had. She remained behind the chair and watched as the two left the haus and entered the barn. She made her way out the haus through the front door and then waited at the side of the haus for the two menner and the boy to enter the haus. She crept around the haus and across the grass to the barn. She opened the door and lo and behold, her promised dochder was there waiting for her beside the square of canvas.

"What is your name, dochder?" Ellen asked the angelic child, stooping own on her haunches beside her.

The child seemed uncertain and so Ellen did not reach out to her, she said only, "I am friends with Able, it will be fine."

"Anna," the child said simply, the finger of her right hand in her mouth, and the corner of the canvas square in her free hand.

"Come with me, Able's mamm wanted me to take you to her."

Anna did not hesitate and soon they were rushing hand in hand across the field to a new life.

Cold hand

Ruth heard the police siren and it was as if a cold hand had gripped her heart. "O Gott, please not again," she prayed out loud, drawing the attention of all the women in her haus. Sissy had so enjoyed the surprise they had arranged for her ahead of the birth of her first boppli, and now the world was again crashing down around Ruth. Mary dropped her cup when a siren came to a stop outside seconds after Ruth had called out. Ruth ran for the door and threw it open. Mary joined her and demanded of the policeman who was running towards them, "Where are my babies?"

"Mrs. Mary Yoder?"

"Jah. Where are they?" Mary repeated.

"Your husband sent word that Anna may have been taken by Ellen Hertzler from the barn on what used to be her property."

Mary pushed past him towards his car, demanding, "Take me to my husband!"

"Three police cars have already gone to the old Hertzler farm. Your husband and Able Beiler followed the direction they believed your daughter to have been taken in," the policeman explained as he drove Mary and Ruth along the dirt road as fast as he could manage.

When they at last reached Amos and Able, they were with a posse of policemen, searching Mr. Raber's orchards. But there was no sign of Anna. Able saw Mary and Ruth and broke away from the group of men, running to them in exasperation. "I told them that she would have taken them to that farm haus past Mr. Raber's haus, but no one will listen," he cried with tears of frustration rolling down his cheeks.

Mary and Ruth and Amos and Able started to run in the direction of the deserted farm haus beyond Mr. Raber's property, and the policeman who, had overheard Able's declaration, instructed three of the officers searching the orchards to follow him as he set off after the four Amish people.

Two officers covered the rear of the house and one kept a lookout for a vantage point from which he could see the entire yard and surrounding area. The policeman in charge walked decisively up to the front door and knocked loudly, declaring, "Mrs. Hertzler, it's the police. Please open the door immediately."

To their surprise, the door opened without undue delay and Ellen stepped aside for them to enter when they asked her permission to do so. The three officers remained positioned outside while the Beilers and Yoders accompanied the policeman inside the haus. Samuel arrived shortly after and barged into the room, surprised at the calm scenario he happened in on. "Where is Anna?" Mary demanded.

Ellen looked surprised at the question. "Anna? Anna

left during her rumspringa. She married Evan and they have kinners they are raising in the Englisch world."

"Nee, Ellen, not that Anna. Mary and Amos's dochder—Anna Yoder!" the policeman corrected her with not a little annoyance.

"Oh." She looked up at Mary and asked in astonishment, "You have a dochder?"

Mary burst into tears and Amos held her tightly to him. The police officer called for a tracker dog to be brought to the haus. Within minutes, Mary had provided the bloodhound with baby Anna's mopping cloth from which to pick up a scent, and the dog had taken off across the yard and into a small outbuilding. The frantic people rushed into the small building to find the little girl fast asleep in a bundle beside the hens' laying boxes. Mary scooped her up into her arms and the little girl smiled contentedly in her sleep and shifted in her mamm's arms.

Back in the arms of the beloved

The relief in the Amish community was palpable. Mary was no worse for wear after her ordeal and Able was lauded as her hero and the person responsible for her being found before any harm could be done to her. He was the proudest big brother around and the bishop assured him that it was not a sin to be proud of saving his schweschder.

Ellen was clearly confused at the mayhem at the haus in which she had spent her childhood. She had lapsed into a severely delusional state by the time she was back in custody and Dr. Susan Stoll had managed to see her. Due to the fact that she had escaped custody, her minimum-security privileges were revoked, and she was sentenced to life imprisonment in an inpatient psychiatric unit with maximum security and no privileges to speak of.

Ellen seemed to live her life in an altered state of reality, so she likely was not aware of the conditions under which she was to spend her remaining years. She flip-flopped from believing she was married and waiting for her husband to fetch her and take her home, to believing she had an angelic dochder at home in the care of her proud daed while she underwent medical treatment to conceive a boppli of their very own to be a baby bruder or schweschder to their dochder.

Meanwhile Doctor Susan Stoll had spent some time back in the Amish community to get to know the circumstances Ellen Hertzler had lived under. If she had any hope of helping the poor disturbed woman, she had to get a grasp of all that had befallen her over the years. Her time back among the Amish, albeit that Ellen's community were a great deal more liberal than the Heuvelton community in which Susan had been raised, had caused her to want to reach out to her Amish family. To that end, she contacted the bishop of the Heuvelton community, who agreed to meet with her. It was the week before Christmas when she drove her car to Heuvelton, dressed in the simplest clothes she had in her wardrobe, and with her hair tied in a knot behind her head. She could make concessions, she was not above trying.

She parked her car outside the house with its ambiguous appearance. Stark white with the typical battleship-gray window frames and doors. No flowerbeds adorned the garden and she remembered how the lawns were always mowed with hand-pushed mowers. She made her way to the door. It was already open and the bishop was in the doorway with a forbidding look on his face, which had aged remarkably since Susan last seeing him. When she thought this through, she came to the realization that it had been a good thirty years since last seeing the mann. She giggled at the comprehension.

He invited her into his living room, where his wife had already placed a tray of eats, a carafe of lemonade, the kaffe pot and two cups. The room was furnished with chairs designed for fellowship, reading the paper or rocking bopplin to sleep, as well as hickory rockers, and wooden benches. She smiled when she spotted the treadle sewing machine, which would always be found by the window in any Swartzentruber home. The dark-colored curtains were hung without curtain rods, with just a string across the widow on which they were now pulled to the side. The living room walls were plain white and no pictures adorned the walls. The only exception to this being a Farmers Co-operative and Feed Store calendar hanging on one wall.

"Miss Stoll, it is gut to see you again after so many long years. You are looking well. The Englisch life has done you gut," the bishop conceded.

"Denke, Bishop Miller." She shocked herself at the ease with which she slipped back into the Pennsylvanian Dutch. "It is gut to be back, and yes, the Englisch world has not been cruel to me. I have kept my faith and live as simple a life as is conducive to me and my profession."

"And what would that profession be, Miss Stoll?" The bishop was always ready to learn of choices made and the lifestyles adopted by those who chose not to remain under the ordnung.

"I am a forensic psychiatrist. I help to determine the mental state of those criminals suspected of being less than mentally healthy," she explained. "I am in fact now Doctor Stoll." She tipped her head at the admission.

"Very good for you, Doctor Stoll. And why is it that you retained your Amish surname?"

"I have never married. I am and always have been Susan Stoll." His look of surprise did not go unnoticed at Susan's words.

"Why is that, Doctor Stoll?"

"As I said before, I have continued to live according to the Amish faith, and no Englisch man I have ever come across could have coped with living in such a way alongside me. I was not willing to become of the Englisch faith and I never met a mann I could have hoped to live as an Amish, albeit in the Englisch world, with certain modern privileges and freedom."

"I would imagine that that would have been very difficult for you. I don't understand your reasons for maintaining the Amish ways since you were never baptized."

"It was not my decision not to be baptized. The ordnung, you and the elders made that decision for me. I have never blamed you for doing so, but I remained in control of my decisions from thereon in and that is how I chose to live my life. I am happy with my decisions. The one regret I have, which is all consuming, is to have been disallowed contact with my family," Susan admitted proudly.

"We can amend that without any further delay," the bishop said, standing up out of his chair. "Come. Your parents and your siblings are waiting to see you again."

Susan could not help but be overwhelmed by the moment. The bishop led her through the haus and out to the community hall at the bottom of the street, where her whole family and their spouses and kinners were gathered. Her daed was confined to a wheelchair, because of age, but her mamm was still upright and dignified. One by one they hugged Susan and there was barely a dry eye in the place. The afternoon was spent catching up the lost years, laughing over the spilt milk and enjoying hearing all the details of the water under the bridge.

Later that night, Susan got to sleep in her childhood bed again. Not since leaving her parents' house had she slept with the sense of sanctity that she did that night, surrounded by family and uplifted by spirituality and a shared sense of acceptance.

Susan spent a traditional Christmas and Epiphany with her family for the first time in very nearly thirty years. It was as if she had never left, with the exception of the new addition of seventeen nieces and nephews who were there this year to share the season with her.

Epilogue

Able rushed up the stairs, dragging his schweschder Anna behind him. At the top of the stairs, he paused and approached the bedroom door solemnly.

"That's okay, Able and Anna, you can come in and meet the new boppli," Mary called from inside the room.

Anna and Able walked in slowly to find Mary sitting up in bed with a swaddled boppli in her arms. The midwife was still packing her bag and Amos was sitting at the edge of the bed, looking as pleased as the proverbial cat who got the cream.

"Is it a bruder or a schweschder?" Able dared ask. "Anna really wants a bruder."

Anna elbowed him in the ribs. "Do not. I have a bruder."

Amos laughed and lifted her onto the bed, patting the space available for Able to also sit where he could better see the boppli. "And what is it that you would like, Able?"

'Oh, you know, as long as the boppli is healthy, it does not matter." He had often heard that said in the community and he thought it the perfect time to try it out.

Amos and Mary laughed at that and the midwife

could not help chiming in. It was then that Able noticed that the cradle was in Mary and Amos's room, and he craned his neck to see that his eyes were not deceiving him.

"There's a boppli in the cradle!" he exclaimed and shot off the bed.

"Two bopplin?" Anna exclaimed with a matching tone.

"Jah," the midwife confirmed. "The mamm and daed knew they could not please both of you with just the one boppli, so Mary very cleverly produced two boppli."

"We have a bruder AND a schweschder?" asked the astonished Able. Beside him, Anna had huge eyes.

"Jah." Mary leaned over to expose the boppli in her arms. "Meet your bruder, Joseph."

With that Amos gently gathered the boppli from the cradle. "And here we have your schweschder. Do you think we should name her, too?"

"Faith," Anna suggested.

Her parents were pleasantly surprised at the name. "That's a lovely name for her, Anna. What do you think, Able?" Mary asked.

"I think that Faith would be the best name for the sibling that managed to give both Anna and me faith in having the bruder and schweschder we wanted."

"We have very clever kinners, here, Mary," Amos laughed.

Life was indeed gut and with Faith and Joseph, the growing family could go from strength to strength… together.

* * * * *

"You don't ever complain. You take care of someone
else's *kinder* without hesitation, and you're giving them a
home they haven't had in who knows how long."

"Trust me. There was plenty of hesitation on my part."

"I do trust you."

Beth Ann's breath caught at the undercurrent of
emotion in his simple answer. "I'm glad to hear that. I got
a message from their social worker this afternoon. She
was supposed to come tomorrow, which is why I stayed
home today to make sure everything was as perfect as
possible before her visit."

"I wondered why you didn't come to the project house
today."

"That's why, but now her visit is going to be the day after tomorrow. What if she decides to take the children and place them in other homes? What if they can't be together?"

Robert paused and faced her. "Why are you looking for trouble? God brought you to the *kinder*. He knows what lies before them and before you. Trust *Him*."

"I try to." She gave him a wry grin. "It's just...just..."

"They've become important to you?"

She nodded, not trusting her voice to speak. The idea of the three youngsters being separated in the foster care system frightened her, because she wasn't sure what they might do to get back together.

"Don't forget," Robert murmured, "as important as they are to you, they're even more important to God." His smile returned. "How about getting some Christmas pie before we have to fish three *kinder* out of the brook?"

With a yelp, she rushed forward to keep Crystal from hoisting Tommy to see over the rail. Robert was right. She needed to enjoy the children while she could.

Don't miss
An Amish Holiday Family *by Jo Ann Brown,*
available November 2020 wherever
Love Inspired *books and ebooks are sold.*

LoveInspired.com

IF YOU ENJOYED THIS BOOK
WE THINK YOU WILL ALSO LOVE

⬡ HARLEQUIN
SPECIAL
EDITION

Believe in love. Overcome obstacles. Find happiness.

Relate to finding comfort and strength in the
support of loved ones and enjoy the journey
no matter what life throws your way.

6 NEW BOOKS AVAILABLE EVERY MONTH!

Oak Hollow, Texas, was supposed to be a temporary
stop between Tess's old life in Boston and the new one
in Houston, which includes her daughter's lifesaving
heart surgery. But when Hannah wraps handsome
police chief Anson Curry—who also happens to be
their landlord—around her little finger, Tess is tempted
for the first time in a long time.

Read on for a sneak peek at
A Sheriff's Star
by debut author Makenna Lee,
the first book in her Home to Oak Hollow series!

"Sweet dreams, little one," he said and stepped out of
the room.

She took off Hannah's shoes and jeans, then tucked
her in for the night. With a bolstering breath, she braced
herself for being alone with her fantasy man.

He stood in the center of the living room, looking
around like he'd never seen his own house. She
followed Anson's gaze to the built-in shelves she'd
filled with precious and painful memories. Things she
wasn't ready to share with him. Before he could ask any
questions, she opened the front door.

"Even though we were coerced, thank you for carrying her home. And for the house tour." Their "moment" in his bedroom flashed before her. *Damn, why'd I bring that up?*

"Anytime." Anson's blue-eyed gaze danced with amusement before he ducked his head and stepped outside. "Sleep well, Tess."

Fat chance of that.

She closed the door to prevent herself from watching him walk away. Tonight, Anson hadn't treated her indifferently like before and, in fact, seemed to be fighting his own temptations. Sometimes shutters would fall over his eyes as he distanced himself, then she'd blink and he'd wear his devil's grin, drawing her in with flirtation. Maybe he wasn't as immune to their attraction as she'd thought.

"I can't figure you out, Chief Anson Curry. But why am I even bothering?"

Don't miss
A Sheriff's Star *by Makenna Lee,*
available November 2020 wherever
Harlequin Special Edition books and ebooks are sold.

Harlequin.com

HSEEXP1020

Love Harlequin romance?

DISCOVER.

Be the first to find out about promotions, news and exclusive content!

Facebook.com/HarlequinBooks

Twitter.com/HarlequinBooks

Instagram.com/HarlequinBooks

Pinterest.com/HarlequinBooks

ReaderService.com

EXPLORE.

Sign up for the Harlequin e-newsletter and download a free book from any series at **TryHarlequin.com**

CONNECT.

Join our Harlequin community to share your thoughts and connect with other romance readers!
Facebook.com/groups/HarlequinConnection

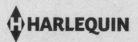